```
302.3 Mur
Murphy, Alexa Gordon.
Dealing with bullying
 #232391107
```

Character Education

Dealing with Bullying

Character Education

Being a Leader and Making Decisions

Being Fair and Honest

Dealing with Bullying

Dealing with Frustration and Anger

Handling Peer Pressure

Handling Teamwork and Respect for Others

Managing Conflict Resolution

Managing Responsibilities

Overcoming Prejudice

Character Education

Dealing with Bullying

ALEXA GORDON MURPHY

INTRODUCTION BY CONSULTING EDITORS
Madonna M. Murphy, Ph.D.
University of St. Francis

and **Sharon L. Banas**
former Values Education Coordinator,
Sweet Home Central School District, New York

Character Education: Dealing with Bullying

Copyright © 2009 by Infobase Publishing

All rights reserved. No part of this book may be reproduced or utilized in any form or by any means, electronic or mechanical, including photocopying, recording, or by any information storage or retrieval systems, without permission in writing from the publisher. For information, contact:

Chelsea House
An imprint of Infobase Publishing
132 West 31st Street
New York NY 10001

Library of Congress Cataloging-in-Publication Data
 Murphy, Alexa Gordon.
  Dealing with bullying / Alexa Gordon Murphy.
    p. cm.—(Character education)
  Includes bibliographical references and index.
  ISBN 978-1-60413-121-5 (hardcover)
  1. Bullying. I. Title. II. Series.
 BF637.B85M87 2009
  302.3—dc22   2008025327

Chelsea House books are available at special discounts when purchased in bulk quantities for businesses, associations, institutions, or sales promotions. Please call our Special Sales Department in New York at (212) 967-8800 or (800) 322-8755.

You can find Chelsea House on the World Wide Web at http://www.chelseahouse.com

Text design by Annie O'Donnell
Cover design by Takeshi Takahashi

Printed in the United States

Bang NMSG 10 9 8 7 6 5 4 3 2 1

This book is printed on acid-free paper.

All links and Web addresses were checked and verified to be correct at the time of publication. Because of the dynamic nature of the Web, some addresses and links may have changed since publication and may no longer be valid.

CONTENTS

Introduction   **7**
by **Madonna M. Murphy, Ph.D.**, professor of education at University of St. Francis, Joliet, Illinois, and **Sharon L. Banas**, former character education coordinator and middle school social studies teacher, Sweet Home School District, Amherst and Tonawanda, New York

1	Bullying Hurts	**13**
2	Understanding Bullies	**25**
3	Understanding Victims	**32**
4	Dealing with Bullying	**41**
5	Bullying in the Media	**54**
6	Bullying in Politics and at Work	**64**
7	Changing the Bullying Culture at Your School	**80**
	Glossary	**93**
	Bibliography	**95**
	Further Resources	**104**
	Picture Credits	**105**
	Index	**106**
	About the Author and Consultants	**110**

INTRODUCTION

On February 14, 2008, as these books were being edited, a shooting occurred at Northern Illinois University (NIU) in DeKalb, Illinois. A former NIU graduate student, dressed in black and armed with a shotgun and two handguns, opened fire from the stage of a lecture hall. The shooter killed five students and injured 16 others before committing suicide. What could have led someone to do this? Could it have been prevented?

When the shooting started, student Dan Parmenter and his girlfriend, Lauren Debrauwere, who was sitting next to him, dropped to the floor between the rows of seats. Dan covered Lauren with his body, held her hand, and began praying. The shield of Dan's body saved Lauren's life, but Dan was fatally wounded. In that hall, on February 14, 2008—Valentine's Day—one person's deed was horrific and filled with hate; another's was heroic and loving.

The purpose of this series of books is to help prevent the occurrence of this kind of violence by offering readers the character education and social and emotional skills they need to control their emotions and make good moral choices. This series includes books on topics such as coping with bullying, conflicts, peer pressure, prejudice, anger and frustration, and numerous responsibilities, as well as learning how to handle teamwork and respect for others, be fair and honest, and be a good leader and decision-maker.

In his 1992 book, *Why Johnny Can't Tell Right from Wrong*,[1] William Kilpatrick coined the term "moral illiteracy" and dedicated a whole chapter to it. Today, as he points out, people often do not recognize when they are in a situation that calls for a moral choice, and they are not able to define what is right and what is wrong in that situation. The California-based Josephson Institute of Ethics agrees with these concerns. The institute states that we have a "character deficit" in our society today and points out that increasing numbers of young people across the United States—from well-to-do as well as disadvantaged backgrounds—demonstrate reckless disregard for fundamental standards of ethical conduct.

According to the 2006 *Josephson Institute Report Card on the Ethics of American Youth*, our children are at risk. This report sets forth the results of a biannual written survey completed in 2006 by more than 36,000 high school students across the country. The compilers of the report found that 82 percent of the students surveyed admitted that they had lied to a parent about something significant within the previous year. Sixty percent admitted to having cheated during a test at school, and 28 percent admitted to having stolen something from a store.[2] (Various books in this series will tell of other findings in this report.) Clearly, helping young people to develop character is a need of national importance.

The United States Congress agrees. In 1994, in the joint resolution that established National Character Counts Week, Congress declared that "the character of a nation is only as strong as the character of its individual citizens." The resolution also stated that "people do not automatically develop good character and, therefore, conscientious efforts must be made by youth-influencing institutions . . . to help young people develop the essential traits and characteristics that comprise good character."[3]

Many stories can be told of people who have defended our nation with character. One of the editors of this series knew one such young man named Jason Dunham. On April 24, 2004, Corporal Jason L. Dunham was serving with the United States Marines in Iraq. As Corporal Dunham's squad was conducting a reconnaissance mission, the men heard sounds of rocket-propelled grenades and small arms fire. Corporal

Dunham led a team of men toward that fire to assist their battalion commander's ambushed convoy. An insurgent leaped out at Corporal Dunham, and he saw the man release a grenade. Corporal Dunham alerted his team and immediately covered the grenade with his helmet and his body. He lost his own life, but he saved the lives of others on his team.

In January 2007, the Dunham family traveled to Washington, D.C., where President George W. Bush presented them with Corporal Dunham's posthumously awarded Congressional Medal of Honor. In the words of the Medal of Honor citation, "By his undaunted courage, intrepid fighting spirit, and unwavering devotion to duty, Corporal Dunham gallantly gave his life for his country."[4]

Thomas Lickona, the author of several books including *Educating for Character* and *Character Matters*, explains that the premise of character education is that there are objectively good human qualities—virtues—that are enduring moral truths. Courage, fortitude, integrity, caring, citizenship, and trustworthiness are just a few examples. These moral truths transcend religious, cultural, and social differences and help us to distinguish right from wrong. They are rooted in our human nature. They tell us how we should act with other human beings to promote human dignity and build a well-functioning and civil society—a society in which everyone lives by the golden rule.[5]

To develop his or her character, a person must understand core virtues, care about them, and act upon them. This series of books aims to help young readers *want* to become people of character. The books will help young people understand such core ethical values as fairness, honesty, responsibility, respect, tolerance of others, fortitude, self-discipline, teamwork, and leadership. By offering examples of people today and notable figures in history who live and have lived these virtues, these books will inspire young readers to develop these traits in themselves.

Finally, through these books, young readers will see that if they act on these moral truths, they will make good choices.

They will be able to deal with frustration and anger, manage conflict resolution, overcome prejudice, handle peer pressure, and deal with bullying. The result, one hopes, will be middle schools, high schools, and neighborhoods in which young people care about one another and work with their classmates and neighbors to develop team spirit.

Character development is a lifelong task but an exciting challenge. The need for it has been with us since the beginning of civilization. As the ancient Greek philosopher Aristotle explained in his *Nicomachean Ethics*:

> The virtues we get by first exercising them . . . so too we become just by doing just acts, temperate by doing temperate acts, brave by doing brave acts. . . . Hence also it is no easy task to be good . . . to do this to the right person, to the right extent, at the right time, with the right motive, and in the right way, that is not easy; wherefore goodness is both rare and laudable and noble. . . . It makes no small difference, then, whether we form habits of one kind or of another from our very youth; it makes a very great difference, or rather all the difference.[6]

This development of one's character is truly *The Ultimate Gift* that we hope to give to our young people. In the movie version of Jim Stovall's book of the same name, a privileged young man receives a most unexpected inheritance from his grandfather. Instead of the sizeable inheritance of cash that he expects, the young man receives 12 tasks—or "gifts"—designed to challenge him on a journey of self-discovery. The gifts confront him with character choices that force him to decide how one can be truly happy. Is it the possession of money that brings us happiness, or is it what we do with the money that we have? Every one of us has been given gifts. Will we keep our gifts to ourselves, or will we share them with others?

Being a "person of character" can have multiple meanings. Psychologist Steven Pinker asks an interesting question in a

January 13, 2008, *New York Times Magazine* article titled "The Moral Instinct": "Which of the following people would you say is the most admirable: Mother Teresa, Bill Gates or Norman Borlaug?" Pinker goes on to explain that although most people would say that, of course, Mother Teresa is the most admirable—a true person of character who ministered to the poor in Calcutta, was awarded the Noble Peace Prize, and was ranked in an American poll as the most admired person in the twentieth century—each of these three is a morally admirable person.

Pinker points out that Bill Gates made billions through his company Microsoft, but he also has decided to give away billions of dollars to help alleviate human misery in the United States and around the world. His charitable foundation is built on the principles that "All lives—no matter where they are being lived—have equal value" and "To whom much is given, much is expected."

Pinker notes that very few people have heard of Norman Borlaug, an agronomist who has spent his life developing high-yielding varieties of crops for third world countries. He is known as the "Father of the Green Revolution" because he used agricultural science to reduce world hunger and, by doing so, saved more than a billion lives. Borlaug is one of only five people in history to have won the Nobel Peace Prize, the Presidential Medal of Freedom, and the Congressional Gold Medal. He has devoted his long professional life and his scientific expertise to making the world a better place.

All of these people—although very different, from different places, and with different gifts—are people of character. They are, says Pinker, people with "a sixth sense, the moral sense." It is the sense of trying to do good in whatever situation one finds oneself.[7]

The authors and editors of the series *Character Education* hope that these books will help young readers discover their gifts and develop them, guided by a moral compass. "Do good and avoid evil." "Become all that you can be—a person of character." The books in this series teach these things and more. These books will correlate well with national social studies standards of learning. They will help teachers meet state standards for teaching social and emotional skills, as well as state guidelines for teaching ethics and character education.

Madonna M. Murphy, Ph.D.
Author of *Character Education in America's Blue Ribbon Schools* and professor of education, University of St. Francis, Joliet, Illinois

Sharon L. Banas, M.Ed.
Author of *Caring Messages for the School Year* and former character education coordinator and middle school social studies teacher, Sweet Home Central School District, Amherst and Tonawanda, New York

---

FOOTNOTES
1. William Kilpatrick. *Why Johnny Can't Tell Right from Wrong,* New York: Simon and Schuster, 1992.
2. Josephson Institute, 2006 *Josephson Institute Report Card on the Ethics of American Youth: Part One – Integrity.* Available online at: http://josephsoninstitute.org/pdf/ReportCard_press-release_2006-1013.pdf.
3. House Joint Resolution 366. May 11, 1994, 103rd Congress. 2d Session.
4. U.S. Army Center of Military History. *The Medal of Honor.* Available online at: www.history.army.mil/moh.html.
5. Thomas Lickona, *Educating for Character: Teaching Respect and Responsibility in the Schools.* New York: Bantam, 1991. Thomas Lickona, *Character Matters: How to Help Our Children Develop Good Judgment, Integrity, and Other Essential Virtues.* New York: Simon and Schuster Touchstone Books, 2004.
6. Richard McKeon, editor, "Nicomachean Ethics." *Basic Works of Aristotle,* Chicago: Random House, Clarendon Press, 1941.
7. Steven Pinker, "The Moral Instinct," *The New York Times,* January 13, 2008. Available online at www.newyorktimes.com.

BULLYING HURTS

> "Many attackers felt bullied, persecuted, or injured by others prior to the attack."
> —U.S. Secret Service and the Department of Education, final report and findings of the Safe School Initiative, 2002

Bullying is not a new problem. Ask your parents and grandparents, and they'll likely be able to tell you stories about bullying from their school days. Just like you, they might have witnessed, experienced, or participated in teasing, pushing, threatening, or other bullying behavior on the school bus, at the playground, or in the locker room.

Kids have teased, harassed, and been downright mean to each other for generations. Until recently, people believed that bullying was just a part of growing up. Adults shrugged off bullying, saying, "Kids will be kids." Kids were left to battle it out among themselves. It was up to them to learn how to survive in the tough world of the schoolyard.

However, attitudes about bullying have changed in the last few decades. Today, bullying is taken much more seriously. Tragedies such as school shootings and suicides carried out by victims of bullying have become more common in the late twentieth and early twenty-first centuries and have brought the negative effects of bullying front and center in schools. Most people now know that bullying is not just a right of passage for kids. It hurts everyone involved: victims, bullies, and even bystanders. And when bullying is tolerated, the community becomes an unsafe place for everyone.

WHAT IS BULLYING?

Everyone has to deal with people they don't like, and not everyone can get along 100 percent of the time. Everyone fights sometimes, but not all conflict between people is bullying. It's important to understand exactly what bullying is and is not, because the best ways to deal with bullying may not work for other types of conflicts.

When is conflict just conflict, and when is it bullying? Dan Olweus, a psychologist who has done extensive research on bullying, was one of the first researchers to make these distinctions and define bullying. According to Olweus, normal

BULLYING: A TIMELESS PROBLEM

To find out how long kids have been bullying each other, one needs only to look as far as a bookshelf. For example, in the classic Charles Dickens novel *Oliver Twist* (1838), the bullying the book's hero experiences seriously affects his life. Oliver Twist is an orphan who spends the first nine years of his life in a home for boys and then moves to a workhouse for adults. There, the other boys taunt and pressure Oliver to ask for more to eat at the end of a meal. When he does, Mr. Bumble, a church official at the workhouse, offers to pay someone five pounds (British currency) to take Oliver away. Oliver is apprenticed to an undertaker. At his apprenticeship, Oliver is taunted and bullied by a fellow named Noah Claypole. Noah continuously taunts Oliver, and one day he insults Oliver's dead mother. Oliver gets angry with Noah and attacks him. Oliver ends up locked in the cellar. Unable to tolerate the way Noah and the undertaker treat him, Oliver runs away the next morning. Oliver's experiences show the serious consequences bullying—and how a person reacts to being bullied—can have.

Bullying Hurts 15

Bullying involves treating someone abusively, either physically, verbally, or emotionally—or all three.

conflict is when two or more people disagree about something—usually something accidental, such as bumping into each other in the hallway or having a misunderstanding. With normal conflict, neither person is trying to get power or control over the other person or get attention.

For example, Charlie and Steve are friends. They made a plan for Steve to come to Charlie's house after school to play video games, but Steve never showed up. The next day, Charlie purposely bumps into Steve in the hallway. "What's your problem?" says Steve. "You blew me off!" says Charlie, giving Steve another little push. The fight escalates until a teacher comes to break it up. Later, when Charlie finds out that Steve had gotten the date mixed up and thought their plan was for Friday, not Wednesday, they resolve the problem. This was poorly handled conflict, but it wasn't bullying.

Bullying is different. According to Olweus, "A student is being bullied or victimized when he or she is exposed, repeatedly and over time, to negative acts on the part of one or more other students." With bullying, the person doing the bullying is purposely trying to hurt the victim—emotionally and/or physically. Whereas the conflict between Steve and Charlie was a onetime event, bullying usually happens repeatedly over time.

Power is an important part of bullying as well. A bully is trying to gain power and control over another student.

THE TRAGIC RESULTS OF BULLYING

In 1999, in Littleton, Colorado, high school students Eric Harris and Dylan Klebold carried out a deadly shooting at Columbine High School before committing suicide. They killed 12 students and a teacher and wounded 28 others before killing themselves. In the aftermath of the shootings, the American public was left looking for answers to why two teenage boys would plan and commit such terrible violence. One possible explanation was bullying.

After the shootings, Columbine students began to talk about the problem of bullying at their school. Some said that Harris and Klebold had been treated as social outcasts at school and taunted for their "goth" or punk-like style of wearing dark clothing and black trench coats. This information led researchers and the media to look more closely at the effects of bullying on its victims and the possible link between bullying and school shootings around the country.

In response to the Columbine shootings as well as others around the United States, the U.S. Secret Service and the Department of Education launched the Safe Schools Initiative to examine the reasons for these attacks. In their final report (2002), they reported that close to three-quarters of students who carry out these attacks have "felt persecuted, bullied, threatened, attacked, or injured by others prior to the incident." Since the Columbine shootings, the problem of bullying has been taken more seriously at many schools across the United States.

Because of this power relationship, emotional reactions to bullying are different from the emotional response in normal conflict. In normal conflict, both people have equal power, and so they might be equally upset about the conflict. With bullying, the bully has power over the victim, and so the bullying is very upsetting for the victim but not for the bully.

THE MANY TYPES OF BULLYING

When most people think of bullying, they picture a child or group of children teasing, throwing things, pushing, or even hitting another child. This kind of bullying is known as direct bullying. Direct bullying can be verbal—name-calling, insulting, teasing, or threatening—or it can be physical—pushing, tripping, hitting, or otherwise attempting to harm the victim physically.

Indirect bullying, on the other hand, is less visible but just as painful to the victim. Indirect bullying is also called "relational" or social bullying. It includes social actions such as purposely excluding someone from a group or spreading rumors about someone. For example, Celia arrives at school one day and no one will talk to her. It seems all her classmates are staring at her and whispering. Even the girls she thought were her friends aren't speaking to her. When she asks a classmate what is going on, she finds out that one of her so-called friends has been spreading rumors that she still wets her bed. The rumors aren't true—but the damage is done. Celia is humiliated and excluded.

Another form of social bullying has emerged with the Internet: cyberbullying. Cyberbullying is when a person is harassed, humiliated, threatened, or tormented by people using the Internet and other interactive technologies such as cell phones. It includes sending multiple insulting or threatening messages to a person's e-mail address or cell phone, creating a Web page for the purpose of humiliating a person, and sharing someone's secrets on public message boards or Web sites. Cyberbullying is an especially powerful form of bullying because it reaches many people at one time and because it can often be done anonymously.

A common myth about bullying is that only boys bully. In fact, both boys and girls bully. Boys tend to use direct forms of bullying, while girls tend to use indirect bullying. According to Olweus, boys tend to target both boys and girls, while girls tend to bully other girls.

Bullying is quite common. A 2001 survey of students in grades 6–10, funded by the Institute of Child Health and Human Development, found that more than 16 percent of students reported having been bullied. Howard Spivak, professor of pediatrics and community health at Tufts University, estimates that a quarter to one-third of U.S. students are involved in bullying, either as a victim or a bully.

HOW BULLYING HURTS VICTIMS

Anyone who has ever been teased, forced to hand over money, or excluded by a group of friends knows how painful bullying is. Many kids get over being bullied—especially if they have the support of family, teachers, and friends. Yet, for many people, bullying can have serious negative effects—both in the short term and the long term.

Bullying can affect how students do in school. Kids who are being bullied regularly may become afraid to go to school. According to the U.S. Department of Health and Human Services, as many as 160,000 kids stay home from school each day because of fear of being bullied. A 2003 survey by the Department of Health and Human Services also found that 5.4 percent of high school students felt unsafe at school or on the way to or from school at least one day in the month before they were surveyed.

Researchers believe that bullying victims may be so stressed out and distracted by bullying that they lose interest in schoolwork. Many victims talk about how being bullied affected their involvement with school. A bullying victim named Hannah reported on the Web site Bully B'ware

SUICIDE ALERT

Sometimes getting bullied can cause such extreme depression that a victim considers—or even attempts—suicide. For example, in 2006, 13-year-old Megan Meier committed suicide after an online bully told her the world would be a better place without her. Megan had been teased in school about her weight, and she suffered from depression. She met a boy named Josh Evans on the social networking Web site MySpace.

At first Megan thought Josh was her friend, but things suddenly changed when Josh wrote to Megan, "I don't like the way you treat your friends, and I don't know if I want to be friends with you." The next day, other students began sending Megan hateful messages, and Josh wrote to her, "The world would be a better place without you." Megan committed suicide shortly after reading this message. Sadly, Megan's parents later learned that "Josh" was actually the mother of a former friend of Megan's (along with an 18-year-old friend) who was trying to find out how Megan felt about her daughter.

Tina Meier holds pictures of her 13-year-old daughter, Megan, who committed suicide as a result of cyberbullying. In her daughter's memory, Meier continues to fight for laws against cyberbullying.

Suicide is never an answer to a problem. It not only cuts a life short, but it also deeply hurts those left behind—parents, siblings, relatives,

(continues)

(continued)

friends, teachers, and classmates. No matter how bad a person may feel, there is always a better way to deal with problems. If you or someone you know has had thoughts of suicide, it's important to talk to a trusted adult immediately. Some warning signs include:

- Talking about suicide
- Thinking or talking a lot about death and dying
- Withdrawing from family and friends
- Giving away belongings
- Saying good-bye to people as if they won't be seen again

Always take these warning signs seriously. It's better to be safe than sorry.

Productions (www.bullybeware.com) that her experience being bullied led her to avoid school and eventually drop out. "After a while it all got on top of me and I avoided school altogether. I made myself ill and never did return back to school," Hannah wrote.

Being bullied can also make social problems worse. Kids who are bullied might have trouble trusting others and developing strong friendships. That's why strong friendships are an important protector against bullies. Victims of bullies often are isolated at school and even stop spending time with their families. Bullying expert Dan Olweus and other researchers have found that teens who are bullied may become aggressive themselves or make the mistake of turning to alcohol or other drugs to help them cope.

The stress of being bullied can even lead to physical problems. Stress is the body's response to a threat—often called the "fight or flight" response. When faced with a threat, a person's body goes into high gear. His or her brain actually sends out a kind of alarm that tells the body to release the

Bullying Hurts 21

hormones adrenaline and cortisol. These hormones help give the body the energy needed to deal with a threat, but they can also have negative effects if a person has too much stress. When a person is bullied over and over for a long time,

How stress affects the body

In stressful situations the hormones epinephrine (adrenaline) and norepinephrine (noradrenaline) act on many parts of the body with dramatic results. Among the changes that take place—immediately, or over time—are the following:

1. Hair may stand on end or even fall out.
2. Stress triggers mental and emotional problems, such as insomnia, headaches, personality changes, irritability, anxiety, and depression.
3. The pupils of the eyes dilate.
4. The output of saliva falls.

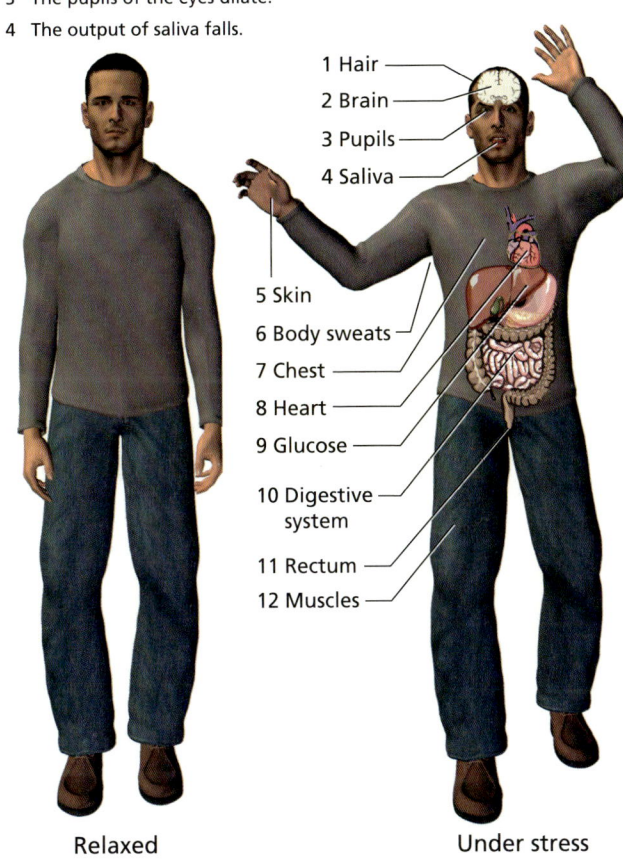

1 Hair
2 Brain
3 Pupils
4 Saliva
5 Skin
6 Body sweats
7 Chest
8 Heart
9 Glucose
10 Digestive system
11 Rectum
12 Muscles

5. The skin turns pale as blood vessels supplying it contract. Also, some people react to stress with outbreaks of skin problems, such as eczema and psoriasis.
6. The body sweats, ready to cool itself if there is great activity.
7. The chest expands, and breathing becomes faster and deeper to deliver more oxygen to muscles.
8. The heart beats faster and harder and blood pressure rises.
9. Glucose is released from the liver to provide food for muscles.
10. The blood supply to the digestive system is diverted and digestion slows.
11. In extreme fear, the bladder and rectum may empty.
12. Muscles tense, ready for fight or flight.

Relaxed   Under stress

© Infobase Publishing

The stress of being a bully's target takes its toll in numerous ways.

the stress can lead to a range of physical symptoms, such as stomachaches, headaches, trouble sleeping, and loss of appetite. Stress can also trigger asthma attacks and make acne worse. It even affects the immune system, which helps the body to fight disease. That's why some people who are bullied may get sick more often.

Most victims of bullying overcome the stress and other problems it causes once the bullying ends. But some—especially those who deal with bullying over a long period of time—end up with lasting mental health problems that affect their lives into adulthood.

One serious mental health problem bullying can lead to is depression. Depression is a serious mental illness. It involves lasting sadness, hopelessness, and despair. People with depression often feel worthless and have trouble believing that things will get better in the future. They often feel tired and lack the energy and spirit to do normal activities. Because of this, depression can affect every part of a person's life. If depression follows a victim of bullying into adulthood, it can affect his or her ability to succeed in a career and have healthy relationships.

The constant stress and fear caused by long-term bullying can also lead to another mental health problem: anxiety disorders. Anxiety disorders include general feelings of uneasiness, panic attacks, phobias (extreme fears of certain things), and post-traumatic stress disorder (PTSD). Anxiety disorders can affect a person's life in many ways, ranging from sleeping problems and moodiness to living in a constant state of fear and avoiding certain places or activities. Like depression, anxiety can make it harder to succeed at work and in relationships.

BULLYING HURTS KIDS THAT BULLY

It may seem like the people who bully others are immune from harm. Kids that bully are often considered popular among their classmates. In fact, a 2000 study by Philip Rodkin found that elementary school boys who are very aggressive may be some of the most popular kids in elementary school classrooms. Because of their bullying behavior, they seem powerful and in control. Yet, bullying can lead to problems for these kids, too.

Even though bullies may seem popular in school, many bullies have trouble trusting others and getting truly close to people—and, as a result, they have few lasting friendships. According to research by The Nemours Foundation's Center for Children's Health Media, even when bullies are popular in middle school, that popularity may begin to drop in high school if they continue to bully. Kids who continue bullying into high school tend to hang out only with other bullies. According to the Substance Abuse and Mental Health

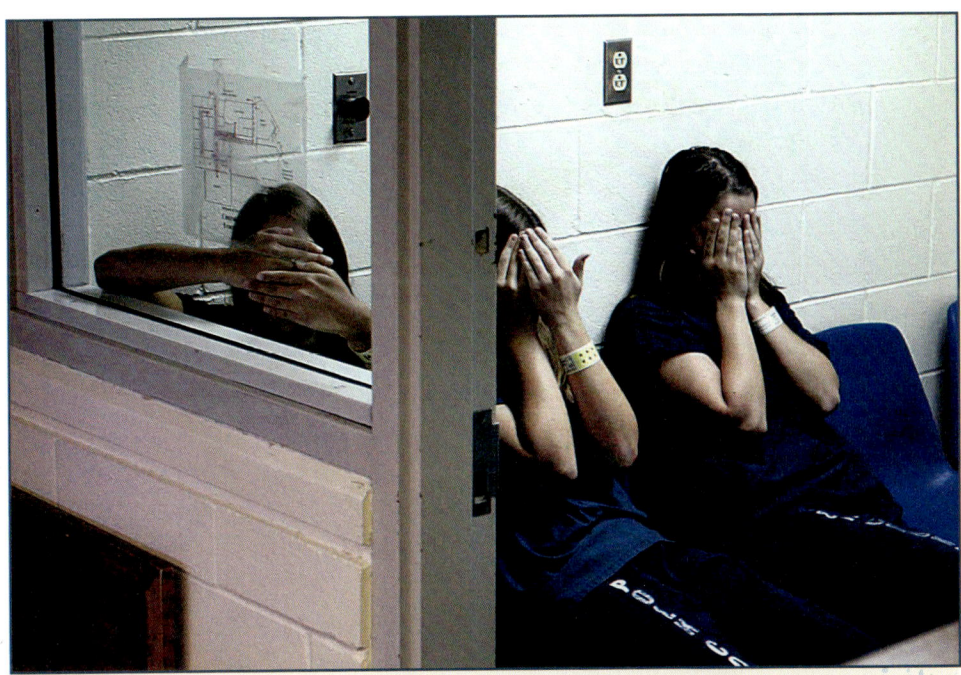

In 2008, seven teens from Bartow, Florida, were charged in the vicious beating of another student. The attackers posted a video of the beating on the popular Web site, YouTube, which helped law enforcement officials identify them. Above, three of the defendants sit in a holding room hiding their faces while waiting to make their individual appearances in court.

Services Administration (SAMHSA), some even get involved in gang activity. Bullies are also more likely to skip school and get into other sorts of trouble, such as vandalism, fighting, and using alcohol and other drugs.

Kids who bully are also more likely to be involved in violent crime as they get older. According to a study by bullying expert Dan Olweus, by age 24, 60 percent of kids who bullied others in school have been convicted of at least one crime. In general, childhood bullies are at greater risk of drug and alcohol abuse, criminal activity, and mental health problems as adults.

If bullies don't learn how to form positive relationships, they may continue to bully others as they get older. They may bully their coworkers, their friends, their partners, and even their own children. Remember the lasting effects bullying can have on victims, and you can see how bullying can become a vicious cycle of hurt if the bully doesn't learn how to treat people with respect.

WHAT ABOUT EVERYONE ELSE?

The effects of bullying don't stop with the victims and the bullies. When bullying is tolerated, it affects everyone. Bullying creates an atmosphere where fear and aggression rule instead of safety and respect. Bystanders—students who witness bullying—may fear walking to and from school or being alone in certain hallways just as much as direct victims of bullying do.

School is a place to learn, make friends, and grow up. Bullying makes it hard for everyone to accomplish these goals. Fortunately, while bullying may be a fact of life, the facts can change. Learning how to deal with—and put a stop to—bullying can help prevent these problems.

UNDERSTANDING BULLIES 2

"I know it sounds horrible, but seeing her cry like that made me feel good. I don't know why, it was like finding a new power."
—Quoted from "Nicky" on the BBC's Real Life Stories "My Bullying Nearly Killed Her"

One national survey found that 13 percent of students in grades 6–10 had bullied others and 6 percent had been both a bully and a victim at some point in time. So, who are these students that bully others? Why would anyone purposely try to hurt someone else, as bullies seem to do?

It was once thought that bullies are really insecure underneath and have low self-esteem (don't feel good about themselves) that they are trying to cover up by bullying others. However, research shows that the opposite may be true. Researcher Dan Olweus found that bullies tend to have very little anxiety, are quite secure, and have positive self-esteem. In other words, bullies are usually confident and feel good about themselves. As discussed previously, bullies tend to be fairly popular in school. According to Olweus, many bullies have a group of two or three friends who support the bullying behavior.

There are specific needs that drive a bully's behavior. Olweus identified three important factors that motivate a bully:

* A need to feel powerful and control others
* Bad experiences at home that lead to the bully wanting to hurt others
* The potential benefit of getting someone's money or making him or her do something

The need to feel powerful may be the most important factor in understanding why kids bully others, because it directly drives bullying behavior. That need is the reason bullies tend to pick on targets who are less likely to fight back and more likely to get upset and be hurt by the bully's actions. They may target kids who are physically smaller than they are, who dress differently or look different in some other way, or who simply have few friends who will stick up for them. When the victim shows that he or she is scared or upset by the bullying, the bully then gets satisfaction out of the victim's reaction and continues to target that victim.

Research shows that bullies often come from families that show little warmth and affection for each other. Their parents may use harsh, sometimes physical, discipline. This teaches young people that it's okay to treat others in this same way. Bullies also report not feeling close to their siblings. All of these factors may contribute to a bully's lack of empathy for others—they don't think about or understand how others feel.

Kids who bully tend to be impulsive and get frustrated and angry easily. Bullies may also have a hard time following the rules and see violence as a good thing. Many bullies learn these values and behaviors at home. Children who live in an angry or violent atmosphere at home are likely to display these same behaviors at school. Troy, a former bully interviewed by writer Donna Smith for iParenting.com, says his father was very tough and he had two older brothers who "terrorized" him. He admits that because he wasn't treated with respect at home, he brought those feelings to school and bullied his peers, whom he saw as "weak" or less powerful.

According to a 1995 *Psychology Today* article by Hara Estroff Marano, many bullies have a kind of paranoia that leads them to assume that others have hostile intentions even when they do not. For example, if someone bumps into a bully accidentally and causes him or her to drop a book, the bully will assume this was done on purpose and be ready to fight. Marano asserts that paranoid bullies " . . . act aggressively because they process social information incorrectly. They endorse revenge."

Researchers have found that many bullies have parents who don't give them proper guidance for positive behavior. This can be through lack of supervision or methods of discipline that are either too permissive, too harsh, or simply not consistent. Researcher Gerald Patterson spent more than 20 years observing parent-child interactions and concluded that children can become bullies when their parents don't consistently respond when they disobey. The parents may ignore the behavior and then, at an unexpected time, lash out harshly at the child. According to Patterson, this pattern actually rewards children for being defiant.

Some kids who bully get little supervision from adults at home. Without that supervision, they may not learn what kind of behavior is acceptable and what is not. Some kids do have a parent around most of the time, but their parents don't discipline aggressive behavior. For example, if a four-year-old pushes his younger sister and the parent doesn't give a clear message that pushing is not okay, the child may grow up thinking that fighting, teasing, and trying to dominate others is okay.

Another important factor that may encourage the bully is peer acceptance. Troy bullied because "it was the cool thing to do" and his peers seemed to look up to him as a powerful figure in and around school. If other kids don't support bullying behavior, bullying very likely would not continue.

Research suggests this view may be enforced by a larger cultural view that being powerful is good and desirable, even if it means hurting others to get there. Television shows, movies, and video games that make entertainment out of humiliating and hurting others may also contribute to the acceptability of bullying behavior in schools.

REACTIVE BULLIES

Some kids that bully do so in response to getting bullied themselves. Researchers call these kids "reactive bullies." Some reactive bullies actually taunt and provoke their tormenters. According to David Perry, professor of psychology

CAN POWER BE POSITIVE?

Bullies want to feel powerful, and that's not necessarily a bad thing. It's the way bullies seek and use power—by hurting others—that's bad and eventually leads to problems for them as well as their victims. Young people with positive social skills and that same desire for power are among the most popular and well-liked kids in school.

Some experts suggest that one way to help bullies turn their behavior around is to teach them positive ways to channel their energy and desire for power. For example, a child who is bullying others may be able to get that same feeling of power by taking on special responsibilities in the classroom or at home. Reformed bullies can even become effective anti-bullying spokespeople in school, get involved in peer conflict resolution, and make other positive contributions. For example, at Mineola High School in New York, the club Increase the Peace has several members who are former bullies. These students received special training to visit elementary and middle schools and teach younger students about accepting differences, reducing prejudice, and preventing bullying.

at Florida Atlantic University, these kids get angry and upset easily and are both easily provoked and provoke others. When a reactive bully has a conflict with another kid, he or she can quickly become aggressive. Similar to the paranoia described earlier, these bullies assume they are being provoked, even when they are not.

Some victims of bullying react by bullying others. For example, Caleb was picked on in elementary and middle school because he was smaller than other boys his age. On the bus, at school, and on the playground, a group of boys would call him names such as "shrimp" and "short stuff" and push him around and even punch him. "It made me feel threatened to the point that I didn't want to go to school," said Caleb in an interview with the author (interviewee's name has been changed to protect anonymity). But eventually, Caleb's frustration with being bullied at school found an outlet. At a summer recreation program, Caleb became friends with another boy, and they began picking on some of the younger kids. "I was really the sidekick, but it made me feel more powerful to turn around and pick on other kids when I had always been the one to be picked on," he said. Eventually, Caleb realized that it was no fun to be on either side of bullying. He later made friends with those kids he had bullied that summer.

WHAT ABOUT RELATIONAL BULLYING?

Most of the research about what makes bullies tick has been focused on the direct bullying in which boys typically engage. Less is understood about the roots of the indirect or relational bullying that is usually perpetrated by girls. Relational bullying is aggression, just like direct bullying, but it's a different kind of aggression. Relational bullies use their social status to control relationships, exclude others, and try to influence how other people act. Relational bullying is different than direct bullying because it is very hard for adults to detect. But it can also be more emotionally harmful than direct bullying.

Most researchers believe that the home lives of kids who become direct bullies do not necessarily mirror the home lives of the kids who become indirect bullies. However, girls' relationship with their parents may contribute to their bullying behavior, but in a different way from how parents of direct bullies do. Psychologist and expert on relational aggression Nicki Crick, Ph.D., has studied relational aggression in girls for more than 20 years. Her research has found that some girls who are indirect bullies may have parents who are very

BULLYING IN THE COURTS

Increasingly, bullying behavior is not tolerated, and some bullies have even faced severe consequences for the way they treat their peers. Bullies might get kicked out school and even have restraining orders—an order from a judge to stay away from a certain person—placed against them. Here are some examples of the consequences some bullies have faced:

* In 2004, three Seattle, Washington, kids who beat up one of their classmates were expelled from school. The victim's parents also sued the school for failing to protect their child.
* A Warren, Pennsylvania, student spent two days in jail for severely bullying his wrestling teammate.
* In 2004, a 14-year-old girl in Scotland obtained a restraining order against a bully at her school.

Bullies aren't the only ones who face consequences. Many students and parents have sued their schools—and even individual teachers or coaches—for failing to protect children from bullying. That's because bullying is increasingly seen as a community problem and not just between the bully and the victim. In other words, schools are considered responsible for keeping students safe—not just from fire and crime but from bullies, too.

jealous and possessive of their children. Crick has also found that these girls are often the family peacemaker; that is, they have the role of keeping the peace when their parents fight. Crick suggests that these findings show that girls who are indirect bullies may learn at home that they have a high level of control over relationships. They use this feeling of power to control relationships among their peers. Crick's research also suggests that relational bullies may behave as they do simply because they think they need to in order to keep friendships and to avoid being excluded themselves.

HELP FOR BULLIES

Help is available for bullies. Once adults identify a child who is bullying, they can also start to address some of the issues that child might be facing at home that could be leading to the inappropriate behavior. Bullies need to have consistent consequences for their behavior to show them that treating other kids in a mean way is not acceptable.

Kids who bully can also learn how to interact with their peers in a positive way and build true friendships. One way adults can help bullies is by helping them build empathy for others—in other words, by helping them learn to think about how other people feel. When a person has the ability to understand the feelings of others, he or she is less likely to do something to intentionally hurt another person.

Some experts suggest that bullies receive structured counseling and/or education to help them learn empathy as well as take responsibility for their actions. In some cases, families can also be involved and parents can be shown how they can create a warm, loving home life with consistent expectations for their children.

Most important, giving bullies a clear message that treating others badly is not okay can help stop bullying before it gets bad. This message needs to come from parents, teachers, bus drivers, coaches, *and* other kids.

3 UNDERSTANDING VICTIMS

"Because of one person, no one talked to me. I became depressed and put myself into isolation. I felt like I was becoming what they said . . . that I was ugly."

—Jade, a victim of indirect bullying, quoted in "Crackdown on schoolgirl bullying epidemic," in The Observer, January 20, 2008

Research by Arizona State University psychology professor Gary Ladd shows that, at the beginning of each school year, close to a quarter of all children are victimized by bullies. But, by the end of the school year, only 8 percent of students are regularly bullied. Ladd calls this a "shopping process": Before students know each other well, bullies "shop around" for people that make satisfying targets.

How does this "shopping process" work? Why do certain kids seem to get consistently targeted by bullies throughout their school years? Researchers have identified a variety of factors that explain why some kids become victims of bullies and some don't.

WHY SOME KIDS ARE SINGLED OUT: EXTERNAL CHARACTERISTICS

Many victims of bullying are first singled out because they look or behave "differently" in some way. Some kids are

Understanding Victims 33

picked on because of their size. They may be younger or physically smaller than most of the other kids—or they may be bigger, taller, or overweight. For example, former U.S.

As a young boy, multiracial golf star Tiger Woods was bullied because of his skin color. Above, Woods at age five plays golf with his father, Earl, who introduced him to the sport.

President Bill Clinton was bullied as a child because he was overweight. TV host and model Tyra Banks was teased in school because she was so tall and skinny.

Some kids are targeted because they have a different ethnic, religious, or cultural background than most of the kids in school or the neighborhood. For example, golf star Tiger Woods was bullied because of his skin color. Woods has a mixed racial background including African-American, Asian, American Indian, and Caucasian ancestors. On his first day of kindergarten, some older boys tied him to a tree and mocked him with racial insults.

Some kids are targeted because they have a special ability or talent that sets them apart. For example, famous singer-songwriter Christina Aguilera was winning talent shows from a very young age. Jealous of her success, her classmates began lashing out at her. She was teased, excluded, and even physically attacked. The bullying got so bad that her family moved to a new neighborhood to get away from it. But you don't have to be a famous performer to get bullied. Some kids may be picked on simply for being good students and making good grades.

Other kids are picked on because they're *not* good at something. Ladd found that some bullying victims aren't singled out until well into the school year. He suggests that something is revealed about these kids in the classroom that attracts bullies. "Something increases their likelihood of being picked on—probably, vulnerabilities in a class environment. Maybe they don't do well in gym, or fumble a reading task," Ladd told *Psychology Today* in 1995.

WHY SOME KIDS BECOME REPEAT VICTIMS: INTERNAL CHARACTERISTICS

Experts agree that most victims of bullying share some common internal characteristics that help explain why bullies not only single them out the first time—but continue to target them over time.

Passive Personalities

Researchers have found that children who are bullied tend to be passive or submissive in social situations. This means that they don't stand up for themselves even when they are not being confronted by a bully. Child psychologist David Schwartz observed children while they were playing. He identified certain children who were passive and submissive. They didn't reach out to others or try to start conversations. When playing with others, they didn't make any demands, requests, or suggestions. For the most part, these children played by themselves rather than with other children.

Schwartz found that these submissive children were the same ones who were eventually targeted by bullies. Their submissive behavior, Schwartz told *Psychology Today*, "seems to mark these kids for later victimization." In other words, bullies see them as easy targets. Remember that bullies are looking to feel powerful and to dominate others, so a submissive peer is a more likely target than one who tends to stand up for him- or herself.

Social Isolation

Typically, victims of bullying are anxious or nervous and insecure. They may also be cautious, shy, and quiet. Researchers have found that bullying victims often have low self-esteem. Perhaps because of their shyness, they tend to have few friends.

Unfortunately, their isolation makes them even more likely to be picked on by bullies. Bullies tend to single out kids who don't have friends who will defend them.

Getting bullied also sets up a vicious cycle of loneliness for victims. Once a young person is known to be a victim of bullying, peers tend to keep their distance. At the same time, the victim may feel ashamed of the way he or she is being treated by the bully, and his or her self-esteem may suffer even more. According to researcher Dan Olweus, victims of bullying often feel "like failures and feel stupid, ashamed, and unattractive." As a result, they may be even more reluctant to participate in after-school activities or try to make friends. As previously noted, many victims are afraid to go to school at all. Unfortunately, withdrawing from others only continues the cycle of loneliness—and bullying.

Passive Response to Bullying

Bullies may pick on many kids in the beginning of the school year, but only an unlucky few continue to be bullied throughout the year. What is it about those remaining few that encourage the bully to keep harassing them? Many experts say that it has a lot to do with how certain kids respond to bullying.

There are three ways people can respond in a conflict. Responding assertively means standing up for yourself without hurting the other person. For example, a child who responds assertively to a bully may simply say, "Leave me alone!" and walk away. Responding aggressively means standing up for yourself in a way that hurts the other person (by accusing or insulting the person or by using violence). A person responding aggressively to a bully may hurl insults back at the bully or try to fight back physically. Responding passively means not standing up for yourself at all. Someone who responds passively to bullying may cry or hand over what the bully asks for.

Most victims of bullying respond to bullies in a passive way. They don't stand up to the bully or try to fight back. Or they may cry and run away—or give in to the bully's demands. For example, they may hand over their money or other possessions if a bully demands it. Unfortunately, responding to a bully in this passive or submissive way only invites the bully to continue to pick on these victims.

Provocative Victims

Some victims of bullying don't fit the profile of the shy, insecure child. Researchers have found that there is another type of victim who may behave in certain ways that provoke

FAMOUS PEOPLE WHO WERE BULLIED AS CHILDREN

In addition to Bill Clinton, Tyra Banks, Tiger Woods, and Christina Aguilera, many other famous people were bullied as children. Here are some examples:

- Singer and actress Demi Lovato left public school to avoid bullying. "Girls were just really vicious," said Lovato. "It was a lot of verbal abuse."
- Actor Christian Bale has beaten up plenty of bad guys as Batman in the movies, but he was severely bullied as a child. "I took a beating from several boys for years," recalled Bale. "They put me through hell, punching and kicking me all the time."
- Singer and actress Whitney Houston remembers being teased about her looks.
- Actor Tom Cruise was a lonely kid with few friends. He also had a learning disability. His family moved around a lot, so he was always the new kid, and he remembers being bullied at every school he attended. "So many times the big bully [came] up and push[ed] me. . . . I'm not the biggest guy," said Cruise.

Bullying encouraged the family of singer and actress Demi Lovato, shown in 2008, to take her out of public school. She's finishing up her high school studies with the help of a tutor.

(continues)

(continued)

* Actress Michelle Pfeiffer remembers running home from school crying because she was teased about her looks.
* Actress Kate Winslet was shy and overweight as a child. She says she endured teasing for two years before the bullying stopped.

All of these former victims of bullying managed to overcome these experiences and lead successful lives.

a bully. Some of these kids may have learning disabilities, such as attention-deficit/hyperactivity disorder (ADHD), that cause them to have trouble concentrating in school and act impulsively, meaning they speak without thinking about the consequences and have strong reactions.

Often, the provocative victim behaves in ways that not only provoke or encourage bullies but also irritate other peers and even teachers. As a result, these victims, while they may seem more outgoing, are still socially isolated. Like passive victims, provocative victims are easy targets for bullies because others are not likely to stand up for them.

Katrina is 10, and she has ADHD. Because of her learning disability, Katrina (whose name has been changed to protect her anonymity) has many behaviors that have provoked bullying. For example, Katrina struggles with social skills. Although she has been taught proper behavior by her parents and therapists, she has a hard time remembering how she should act in certain situations. Katrina says she has "all these thoughts in my head" that she can't shut off or tune out. This makes it hard for her to concentrate and remember how to act. She often stands too close to others and makes them uncomfortable. She has exaggerated reactions to things—something that makes other kids giggle may make Katrina roll on the floor laughing hysterically. Kids often pick on her when she eats because she holds her fork "like a shovel" and chews and talks with her mouth open. Katrina has been taught table manners, and she doesn't mean to act this way, but her learning disability makes it hard for her to remember to act that way in the moment. This makes her irritating to her classmates and an easy target for bullies.

According to a national survey on school discipline conducted by Children and Adults with Attention-Deficit/Hyperactivity Disorder (CHADD), 32 percent of kids with ADHD are actually encouraged by their peers to act in disruptive ways that will get them in trouble. Many adults assume that children with ADHD are bullies because they behave in aggressive or disruptive ways. Yet, in the same study by CHADD, researchers found that these students were often victims of bullies first and reacted in an aggressive way. So although they were not truly bullies, they got into trouble because of the way they reacted to being bullied.

TERESA'S STORY

Teresa* was a victim of indirect bullying. When she was in school, the girls who sat at the "popular" table used to stare at her and point and laugh at her during lunch. "So much so that I usually couldn't eat," says Teresa, who was interviewed by the author.

The teasing and excluding went on for the entire school year. "I never did anything to deserve the teasing," she said. "I was shy. My mom dressed me in clothes that were different from what other kids wore. I wanted desperately to fit in, but just didn't know how. I didn't understand what I was doing wrong. I didn't have the self-esteem to fight back."

Because of the ongoing teasing, Teresa's parents withdrew her from school and enrolled her in a private school the following year.

*Teresa's name has been changed to protect her anonymity.

If victims act passively or behave in ways that seem to "invite" bullies to pick on them, does that mean that bullying is their fault? Of course not, but many victims blame themselves. If a person is shy, passive, or has few friends, it doesn't mean he or she has done something wrong. The bully is hurting other people—and that is wrong. However, if a person is being bullied, he or she can learn positive social skills that will provide some protection from bullying.

HELP FOR VICTIMS

Like bullies, victims may have underlying problems that can be addressed to help them overcome the pain of being bullied. They can learn how to act more assertively and confidently in general, so that bullies don't see them as easy targets. Sometimes, therapy or counseling can help with the feelings of anxiety, insecurity, and low self-esteem that may lead to bullying and are made worse by bullying. Most important, all young people should feel confident that their peers, teachers, and parents will not tolerate bullying. No one should feel that they "deserve" to be bullied or that they are not worth others sticking up for them. A positive community can go a long way in preventing and defusing bullying.

DEALING WITH BULLYING 4

> "When a resolute young fellow steps up to the great bully—the world—and takes him boldly by the beard, he is often surprised to find it comes off in his hand, and that it was only tied on to scare away the timid adventurers."
>
> —Ralph Waldo Emerson (1803-1882), poet and essayist

When young people are faced with bullying, they often feel helpless—as if there is nothing they can do to stop the bullying. Many victims of bullying try to give in to a bully's demands in hopes that the bully will leave them alone. But this cooperation only encourages the bully. Yet, there are things you can do to stop bullying—even before it starts.

BE CONFIDENT

Bullies tend to single out kids who seem unsure of themselves. Therefore, one of the most effective ways to ward off a bully is to act confident. If a bully sees that it's easy to make a person feel bad, he or she will keep trying because that's the result bullies are after. But if a target communicates—through words, actions, and body language—that the bully can't hurt him or her, often the bully will back off.

One way to showcase your confidence is through body language. With proper body language, others can often tell how you feel by the way you stand and walk, as well as by your facial expressions and what you do with your hands. A person who feels confident walks with his or her head held high and back straight. Confident people also make more eye contact with others and keep their hands away from their faces.

On the other hand, people who are unsure of themselves may walk with their shoulders hunched and look down at the ground to avoid making eye contact with others. They may cover their mouth with their hands or seem to fidget a lot, as if they don't know what to do with their hands. This body language communicates the opposite of confidence—and can even communicate fear. This is exactly the kind of body language that invites a bully's attention.

The best way to communicate confidence is to build self-esteem so that you actually feel confident. Positive self-esteem is important for everyone to have. A person with good self-esteem feels that he or she is worth caring about and deserves respect. Self-esteem gives you the confidence to try new things and make good decisions. When you have positive self-esteem, a bully's insults bother you less because you have enough confidence in yourself to know that what the bully says doesn't matter. Good self-esteem also gives you the confidence to deal with bullying without fear.

Good self-esteem can come from many sources. When family members, teachers, and coaches help you accomplish a goal, encourage you to keep trying when you're faced with a challenge, or point out your strengths, this can all boost your self-esteem. You can also play a hand in boosting your own self-esteem. Here are some ways to do that:

- **Know your strengths.** Everyone is good at something. Write down everything you're good at. It may be playing tennis, taking photographs, or baking cookies.

- **Challenge yourself.** Think of some things you'd like to learn how to do. Then, make a plan with your parents for tackling these goals. You'll feel great when you accomplish them.
- **Compliment yourself.** Each day, notice when you did something well and give yourself a pat on the back.
- **Develop positive body image.** Body image is how you view your body. It's easy to compare your size and shape to others and decide that you're not "perfect." But the truth is, the "perfect" body is something that isn't real. If you feel good and your health-care provider thinks you're healthy, that's all you should worry about. Appreciate your unique looks, shape, and size and try not to compare yourself to others.
- **Be alert for negative thoughts**. It's easy to let negative thoughts creep into your head, telling you you're not good enough and making you feel low. Be alert for these self-esteem killers and turn your negative thoughts into positive ones. For example, if you catch yourself thinking "I knew I wouldn't get an A on that test. I'm stupid," stop yourself and turn the thought into a positive one: "I worked really hard and I pulled my grade up from last time. Next time, I'll try to do even better."

GET INVOLVED

A great way to build confidence and meet other kids who you may have things in common with is by joining a school or community group. Find out what activities are offered at your school by checking the school Web site or talking to a guidance counselor. You can also find out about groups or activities outside of school, through a church or community center. If you're not sure what to join, think about your interests. For example, you may find a group, club, or activity that focuses on your interest in:

- **Music**—If you sing or play an instrument (or want to learn), consider joining the school or community choir or band. You can also find smaller groups to join. Singers may like an a cappella group, and musicians may connect well with a smaller jazz ensemble. If there are no smaller groups, talk to the chorus or bandleader about forming one.
- **The outdoors**—Some areas may have a hiking or outing club that will let you explore the great outdoors with others your age.
- **Academics**—Join your school's science, math, or literary club to meet up with others who love these subjects and want to take their learning beyond the classroom.
- **Sports**—Even if you're not into team sports, you may make great friends, have fun, and stay in shape on the tennis court, the golf course, the cross-country trail, or with other competitive sports groups at your school.

You don't have to join a club or a sport in order to get involved and make friends. There are many other ways to participate in school activities: volunteer to help decorate the gym for the school dance, participate in cleaning up your local park, help organize the student elections, write for your school newspaper, help out with fund-raising for a class trip—the possibilities are endless.

Even if you're not usually a "joiner," consider finding a group that interests you, or start one yourself. In addition to helping you make friends, spending time on something you enjoy is rewarding and can build your confidence—another important way to protect yourself against bullies.

FRIENDSHIP IS THE BEST PROTECTION

If bullying is a problem at your school—and especially if you've had problems with a bully in the past—avoid being alone in places where a bully may target you. Find at least one friend that you can walk to and from school or the bus stop with, eat lunch with, and hang out with on the playground. Even a bully who has bothered you in the past may be less likely to bug you if he or she can't catch you alone. Plus, a good friend can boost your self-esteem and remind you that you're a likable person who deserves respect.

Choose your friends carefully, however. Some kids may seem to include you, but that doesn't mean they are good friendship candidates. For example, it may be tempting to hang out with someone who invites you to skip school with him or her. Or, you may feel happy to be included if a classmate shares a rumor with you about another kid. But kids who pressure you to do things that hurt yourself or others are not good friends. They don't respect others—and eventually they'll show that they don't respect you, either. Instead of trying to fit in with the "cool" kids, seek out friends who share your values and interests. Remember that a good friend will never pressure you to do something you don't want to do—or purposely exclude you from a group.

A good place to start finding good friends is in the activities and clubs discussed earlier. Look for opportunities in other places, too. Maybe you can ask a friend from science class if he or she wants to have lunch. Or invite a new kid to join your basketball game. Learn to be friendly and open-minded—and you may find a great friend in an unexpected place.

HOW TO HANDLE A BULLY

So far, you've read about ways you can protect yourself from being bullied by building your self-esteem and making friends. But what if a bully singles you out anyway? In this section, you'll learn what to do about being bullied.

First, stay calm. Try not to let the bully see you get upset. This will only encourage the bully to continue because that's the reaction he or she wants. Try to stay calm instead of crying or getting angry or flustered. This isn't always easy in the moment. Taking deep breaths and silently telling yourself, "I can handle this," can help.

Be assertive. Remember, that means standing up for yourself without fighting. You don't want to make the bully angry or cause the fight to escalate. You just want to stand up for yourself and get the bully to leave you alone. This is also where your confident body language is helpful. Hold your head up and keep your back straight. Look the bully calmly in the eye. Practice some simple one-liners, such as "Leave me alone" or "Cut it out." If you feel safe, use one of these and then calmly walk away. But remember that your safety is most important. If you're afraid the bully may hurt you, quickly move away from the bully and head to a place where there are adults around.

Don't start exchanging insults with a bully. This will only lead to more insults and possibly physical fighting. Ten-year-old Katrina, who has ADHD, deals with a lot of bullying at her school. She says that when kids try to counter by teasing a bully back, this only causes the bullying to continue. "They usually brush it off and tease you with worse names. The only thing you can do is think of worse names than they think of. Sometimes you win and sometimes not so much." Remember, your goal is to make the bullying stop. That's the only true way to "win" in a bullying situation. Try to come up with ways to respond to a bully that won't leave an opening for him or her to respond in a worse way to you.

If you are bullied, be sure to tell an adult. If it's important to you, ask him or her to keep the conversation between the two of you, but know that if you are in real danger, the adult may feel a responsibility to help you. This person can help you figure out what to do about the bullying. If the first person you tell doesn't think anything needs to be done and you disagree, keep telling people until you find someone who takes you seriously. Remember that it is your school's job to

WHAT TO DO IF YOU ARE BULLIED ONLINE

If you are being bullied on the Internet, don't respond to the harasser. If you can, block the person bullying you from sending you e-mails, instant messages (IMs), and text messages. Be sure to save all evidence of the bullying: Print out any e-mails, messages, or Web sites so you can show an adult. Then tell a parent or another adult about the problem. Nancy Willard, executive director of the Center for Safe and Responsible Internet Use, suggests the following steps for dealing with cyberbullying:

- Identify the bully, if you're not sure who it is. Contact your Internet service provider to see if they can help you track down the source of the e-mails and IMs.
- Contact the school if the bullying is being done by a fellow student or through school computer systems.
- File a complaint with the cyberbully's Internet service provider, cell phone provider, or Web host. Cyberbullying is against the terms of use of most of these service providers.
- Contact the bully's parents. Often the parents have no idea what their child is up to. Willard suggests sending the parents a letter describing the problem, with copies of all e-mails or other evidence of the bullying.
- Take legal action. In some cases, your parents may want to have an attorney send a letter to the bully's parents or even file a lawsuit to put a stop to the cyberbullying. In cases where cyberbullying crosses the line to criminal activity (for example, if you are threatened with violence), the police may need to get involved.

Take steps to protect yourself from cyberbullying and other Internet crimes. Don't give out personal information—such as your full name, address, or phone number—on public Internet sites. If anything you see or read online makes you uncomfortable, tell a parent or another trusted adult.

protect all students from bullying and other harm. If bullying is allowed to continue, it hurts you, the bully, and others around you.

Many students are afraid to tell on a bully for fear of being called a "tattletale" and making the bullying problem worse. Yet, keeping silent about bullying only sends the message that bullying is okay. Many schools today have special rules and programs in place to deal with bullying, and adults know effective ways of handling it. Don't be afraid to tell on a bully—no one should have to put up with being treated badly.

Once you tell a parent or another adult, a number of things may happen to deal with the problem. Your parents may meet with you teacher(s), school counselor, and other school officials. Sometimes, your parents may talk directly to the bully's parents. Often, you will have a meeting at school with your parents, the school counselor, and the bully and his or her parents. The consequences for the bully depend on the situation and the school's policies. The important thing is that the bully gets the message that bullying is not okay and that he or she won't get away with it any longer.

BYSTANDERS: DON'T JUST STAND BY AND WATCH

When it comes to bullying, there is no such thing as an innocent bystander. Students can either be a part of the solution and help put a stop to bullying in your school, or they are part of the problem. In fact, bystanders can play a very important role in either stopping a bully or encouraging him or her to continue. One study by Hawkins, Pepler, and Craig (2001) found that 57 percent of the time, when bystanders step in and stand up for the victim, the bullying stops within 10 seconds.

Bullying usually happens away from adults—between classes, on the playground, or after school. Often the only witnesses are other kids, and much of the time, they stand by and

BULLYING AND THE LAW

One result of adults taking bullying more seriously is that many states have passed anti-bullying legislation in recent years. Most of these laws require schools to have a policy against bullying in place. Many of them also require or encourage schools to have a bullying prevention program in place. That means they must take steps to stop bullying from happening before it becomes a problem. Anti-bullying legislation also covers issues such as discipline requirements

(continues)

Arlington High School assistant principal Jennifer Young holds a collection of confiscated cell phones in September 2007. After students at the Texas school were caught bullying in text messages, the school began a policy of banning students' cell phones on campus. If students are caught using them, the phones are held and can only be returned after students pay a $15 penalty.

(continued)
for students who bully and who is required to report bullying to authorities.

Anti-bullying laws are not without controversy. The organization National School Safety and Security Services (www.schoolsecurity.org) argues that laws specifically addressing bullying are not necessary since bullying behavior is already covered by school safety and antiharassment laws already in place. Others say that many anti-bullying laws don't go far enough in protecting students from bullying. The watchdog group Bully Police USA keeps tabs on state anti-bullying laws and grades them A–F. To find out if your state has a law against bullying and whether it makes the grade, check out www.bullypolice.org.

watch the bullying without doing anything. They may not like it, but they usually don't do anything to stop the bully or help the victim. They either don't know what to do or are afraid that if they defend the victim, they'll be targeted by the bully next. Yet bullying affects bystanders, too. Passively watching bullying can make students feel helpless and even guilty. It can also make students feel unsafe and worried that they'll be a victim of the bully next. Taking steps to stop a bully, on the other hand, not only helps the victim, it helps you and all of your classmates feel safe. It can also make you feel great to realize that you are not powerless against the school bullies.

Some bystanders don't stand passively by; they actively encourage the bullying. In cases of direct bullying, they may do this by cheering the bully on, laughing, or even adding taunts of their own. In cases of indirect bullying, not-so-passive bystanders may help spread a rumor about someone or join with the bully in excluding someone from a group. Behavior like this not only helps the bully but it also crosses the line toward bullying itself. Even if you didn't initiate the

INJUSTICE IS EVERYONE'S PROBLEM

Whether you are a passive or not-so-passive bystander, it can take courage to do something about bullying when you see it. You may feel that since you are not being bullied, it's not your problem and so it's not up to you to do anything about it. You may also be afraid of appearing "weak" by standing up for a victim of bullying. But it takes strength to go against the flow and stand up for what's right—especially when you're doing it on behalf of someone else.

Consider all the white people who participated in the civil rights movement alongside black Americans in the 1960s. Many of them put their lives on the line standing up for what they believed was right. In the summer of 1964, for example, hundreds of white civil rights workers came to Mississippi to help with black voter registration. Although blacks had the right to vote, the white supremacist group the Ku Klux

(continues)

SCHWERNER   CHANEY   GOODMAN

During the civil rights movement, bullying and intimidation sometimes turned deadly for people looking to aid blacks. In June of 1964, Mississippian James Chaney, 21, and New Yorkers Michael Schwerner and Andrew Goodman, 20 and 24, respectively, worked to register black voters in Mississippi, against the wishes of some locals. Members of the KKK, who opposed their actions, beat them to death, in part, to bully others into not doing the same thing.

(continued)

Klan (KKK) used brutal methods to stop them from exercising that right. Three civil rights workers—James Chaney, Andrew Goodman, and Michael Schwerner—were murdered by members of the KKK that summer. Do you think people like Chaney, Goodman, and Schwerner—and the countless others who risked their safety to ensure that black Americans had the freedom to vote—are remembered as weak for fighting for the rights of the less powerful? Just the opposite; they are remembered as brave and strong. They weren't afraid to take a risk to stand up for what's right.

bullying, you are just as guilty as the bully if you participate in this way. You may think that supporting a bully this way will win you his or her friendship, protect you from getting bullied, or make you popular. However, all you're really doing is perpetuating the bullying problem at your school—that hurts you, your so-called friends, and the victims of bullying. Your social life—and your future—will be better served by making true friends and steering clear of the school bullies.

Once you gather the courage to help stop a bully, what can you do? Sometimes it's as simple as telling the bully "Leave her alone." If the bully is a friend of yours, it can be particularly effective to just tell him or her to stop. When he or she sees that you—and other students—don't condone the actions, the bully may just back off.

If you don't feel it's safe to say something to the bully, walk away and find an adult. Tell the adult what's going on and ask him or her to come help. It may feel like "tattling," but it's always okay to tell when someone is getting hurt. Remember that bullying hurts on the inside even if the victim isn't being physically hurt on the outside. Telling an adult is always the right thing to do.

Another great way to help out when you see bullying is to be kind to the victim. Remember that kids who get bullied often have few friends, and this makes them more likely to get bullied. Approach the person being bullied. Ask if he or she is okay. Befriending a victim of bullying can help protect him or her from getting picked on again and give him or her the confidence to stand up to bullies in the future.

If someone in your group of friends is indirectly bullying someone by spreading rumors or excluding that person, don't go along with it. Tell the friend that his or her behavior is not okay with you. Don't help spread rumors. Again, make a point to be kind to the person getting bullied. Often indirect bullying can cause even deeper pain to the victim than direct bullying. Be a friend to that person and let him or her know you don't believe the rumors being spread or that you don't agree with what the bully is doing.

Bystanders can also help by encouraging victims of bullying to report the problem to an adult. Offer to go with the person and share what you witnessed. Try to get other classmates who witnessed the bullying involved as well. Remember that stopping the bully helps everyone in your school feel safe—including you. Bullying is not just the victim's problem—it's a school's and a community's problem.

5 BULLYING IN THE MEDIA

"If you came and you found a strange man . . . teaching your kids to punch each other, or trying to sell them all kinds of products, you'd kick him right out of the house, but here you are; you come in and the TV is on, and you don't think twice about it."

–Dr. Jerome L. Singer, Yale University
professor emeritus of psychology

Obviously, bullying is not just a problem between the bully and his or her target. Bystanders to bullying—that is, other kids who witness bullying—have a big influence on whether bullies are encouraged or discouraged. Unfortunately, all too often, bullies are cheered on by their peers with laughter, encouragement, or even silent acceptance. Why is it so easy for so many young people to accept bullying as a part of their school experience—and even in some cases find it amusing or entertaining to watch a peer get bullied? Furthermore, why have the consequences of bullying been largely ignored by adults for so long? In other words, why is bullying largely accepted in our society as normal behavior?

One major influence on young people's attitudes and behavior is arts and entertainment directed at them:

television, movies, music, and video games. Many research studies have shown a link between violence on television and violent and aggressive behavior in young people. According to the American Academy of Child and Adolescent Psychiatry, even watching one violent show can increase a child's tendency to act in an aggressive way. Some research has shown that when someone is angry or frustrated before watching violence on TV, or becomes angry or frustrated about something immediately afterward, he or she is more likely to behave in violent or aggressive ways.

The influence of violent TV can be even stronger than the influence of a young person's parents and other family members. Research shows that watching violent TV shows can increase a child's violent behavior even when the atmosphere at home is not violent or aggressive.

Television watching not only has an influence on violent and aggressive behavior in general, but it has also been linked directly to bullying. A 2005 study by researchers at the University of Washington's School of Public Health found that preschoolers who watch a lot of television are more likely to become bullies later on in life. During the study, researchers found that the risk of becoming a bully in elementary school increased with the number of hours of TV four-year-olds watched per day. Those who were found to be bullies in grade school had watched an average of five hours of TV per day. Another study found that teens who watch more than one hour of TV per day are more likely to be aggressive or violent as adults. On the other hand, according to the organization Common Sense Media, reducing the TV and video game time of third- and fourth-graders to less than one hour per day can decrease verbal and physical aggression by nearly one-half.

The University of Washington study did not consider what shows the preschoolers watched, but the study's author, Frederick Zimmerman, told the *Seattle Times*, "Kids' TV often has a particularly bad kind of violence—the humorous kind." Many shows directed at families and children portray violent and

56   DEALING WITH BULLYING

aggressive behavior as funny or entertaining. For example, in the popular cartoon *SpongeBob SquarePants*, SpongeBob and his friends often resort to physical violence to solve problems. They also often speak rudely and tease one another. Yet, no one seems affected by the violence or teasing.

Still, violence on TV is common. According to Common Sense Media, two out of three TV shows contain violence. The organization also reports that children who watch two hours of cartoons a day may see 10,000 violent acts a year. In

SpongeBob SquarePants writer Stephen Hillenburg poses with the title character, SpongeBob, in 2006. The popular cartoon often depicts SpongeBob and his friends using physical violence to solve problems, as well as teasing and insulting among characters. These actions are shown as being humorous, which can have negative effects on impressionable viewers.

fact, TV directed at children contains twice as many violent acts than programming for adults. Put it all together, and it's easy to see how TV contributes to the problem of bullying and aggression among young people.

Even TV shows that aren't violent can promote aggressive or simply mean behavior. For example, the audition phase of *American Idol*, a popular reality/singing-competition show, involves the judges dishing out harsh criticism and often openly laughing at contestants who are untalented. While we see the contestants' initial reaction, we don't see how the harsh criticism and subsequent public ridicule affects them in the long term. Other reality TV shows encourage contestants to go behind each other's backs and gang up on one another in order to eliminate other players and get ahead.

On the TV show *America's Funniest Home Videos*, viewers' home movies are aired. Many of the videos show people having various mishaps, such as falling off a bicycle, getting hit with a baseball bat, or slipping. Encouraging children to laugh at other people's mishaps on TV may teach them to laugh at the mishaps of real people—and these aren't always funny. For example, if a student trips and falls on the stairs, many students may laugh and even make fun of the person. While it may seem funny to others, the person could be hurt and is probably embarrassed. A more appropriate response would be to see if the person is okay first, and then perhaps laugh it off *with* the person—not at him or her.

According to the American Academy of Child and Adolescent Psychiatry, violence on TV can influence a child's attitude about violence in real life in a number of ways. First, watching characters solve problems with physical violence, or insult or tease each other with little or no consequence, can desensitize young people to the very real and very serious effects of violent and aggressive behavior. It can also help teach young people that violence is an acceptable way to solve problems in real life and that it is okay to imitate the aggressive behavior they see on TV. For example, when

DEALING WITH BULLYING

American Idol judges Paula Abdul and Randy Jackson pose with former contestant William Hung (*right*) at Nickelodeon's 17th Annual Kids' Choice Awards in California in 2004. *American Idol* draws a lot of attention from episodes that feature rejected auditioners whose skills are often made fun of by one or more of the judges. Hung is one of the TV show's most popular "rejects."

children see the characters on *SpongeBob SquarePants* teasing and insulting each other with little reaction or consequence, they may come to think it's okay to talk to their own peers this way. Yet, in reality, talking to each other this way is hurtful and demeaning.

BECOMING MEDIA LITERATE

One way to combat the effects of watching violence on TV is by becoming media literate. That means that you don't just

VIDEO GAMES AND BULLYING

Research shows that violent video games also increase aggressive behavior in young people. Several studies have found that playing violent video games increases a person's aggressive thoughts, feelings, and behavior. Research also suggests that because the games are interactive, the effects may be even stronger than watching violence on TV. Players are encouraged to play the role of aggressive characters and actively participate in violent acts in order to win the game. Dr. Craig Anderson, a psychological researcher, told the American Psychological Association: "Violent video games provide a forum for learning and practicing aggressive solutions to conflict situations."

Some video games are extremely violent but don't show any blood, so young people, parents, and even policy makers think they're age-appropriate. For example, some violent video games are rated "E" for "everyone" because the violence is cartoonish or fantastical. In some ways these depictions can be even more damaging because they make it seem as though being violent causes no real harm. According to Anderson, research has shown a link between increased aggression and E-rated violent video games.

It has been learned that some students who carried out school shootings played certain violent video games, which has led to speculation that playing such games can influence a person to commit extreme violent acts. For example, the shooters in the Columbine Massacre were known to have played violent video games such as Doom, Redneck Rampage, and Duke Nukem. It appeared, from journals and videotapes made by shooters Eric Harris and Dylan Klebold that were found after the attack, that the teens planned the attack with these games and some violent movies in mind. The family of one of the victims in the attack tried to sue several video game distributors, but the lawsuits were dismissed in the name of free speech. It is difficult to conclude that in any one incident a violent video game is to blame, but research does show that playing violent video games can increase aggression—especially in players who already have aggressive tendencies, according to Anderson.

accept what you see on TV at face value. Instead, you watch TV with a critical eye, asking questions and making your own judgments about what you see. Becoming media literate helps you to be a responsible citizen. It makes you a wiser consumer and more thoughtful person about the world around you.

A person who is media literate asks questions about what he or she sees on television and in movies. When you see a violent act or aggressive or mean behavior on TV or in the movies, stop and think about it. Asking the following questions can help you to better understand the real message behind what you're watching.

- **What are the consequences?** Many TV shows and movies show violence or aggression with no real consequences—that is, no one gets seriously hurt or seems emotionally affected by the violence. When you see aggression and violence on TV, ask yourself what the consequences would be if a similar incident happened in real life. Would anyone be seriously injured? Would they get into trouble, or would their behavior be considered acceptable by police, parents, or school authorities? Considering these questions reminds you that much of what is shown on TV is unrealistic.
- **How are conflicts resolved?** Be alert for conflicts on TV and in movies. How are they resolved? If they're resolved by fighting or exchanging insults (even if humorous), think about a better way the characters could have dealt with the conflict.
- **Do you like the characters?** Consider which characters are portrayed as likable and which are not. Are the victims of aggression and violence people you sympathize with? Or do they seem to "deserve" the treatment? What about the characters who are acting aggressively?

THE HUMANITAS PRIZE

For all the violence and disrespectful treatment shown on TV, many shows promote positive social values such as respect and tolerance. The Humanitas Prize is awarded every year to screenwriters who create feature films or television programs that "affirm the dignity of the human person, probe the meaning of life, and enlighten the use of human freedom." Some recent winners of the Humanitas Prize include:

2006
Children's Animation: Miss Spider's Sunny Patch Friends: A Froggy Day in Sunny Patch
Children's Live Action: Edge of America
Feature Film: Crash

2007
Children's Animation: Jakers! The Adventures of Piggley Winks: "The Gift"
Children's Live Action: Molly: An American Girl on the Home Front
Feature Film: Freedom Writers and Venus

Freedom Writers, featuring Oscar winner Hilary Swank and R&B star Mario, won a Humanitas Prize in 2007. The film is about students who find strength to make positive change through writing stories. Above, cast members pose in a scene from the film.

- **Is this realistic?** Would this kind of action happen in "real life"? If it did, what would the consequences be? Are the characters realistic, and do you know people who really act like that? Have you seen conflicts resolved in similar ways?
- **How would you feel?** Consider how you would feel if you were in the shoes of the character being insulted or physically assaulted. How would you want to be treated instead? Sometimes violence seems less entertaining when you put yourself in the shoes of the characters.

Also, be alert for ways that people are stereotyped or made fun of in the way that they're portrayed in the media. This can be harder to pick up on. For example, are pretty, blond characters portrayed as being silly or less intelligent? Are overweight characters portrayed in a negative way? These kinds of messages are important because they help promote prejudice and intolerance—two enemies of a respectful, bully-free community.

Make a point of asking yourself these questions anytime you see fighting or aggressive behavior on TV or in a movie. Talk about them with a parent or a friend. After a while, it will become second nature to view entertainment with a critical eye. You may even notice ways that TV and movies are influencing the way your classmates treat each other.

WHAT IS BEING DONE ABOUT VIOLENCE ON TV?

With so much evidence linking violence on TV to violence, bullying, and aggression in young people, a number of actions have been taken in recent years to reduce children's exposure to violence on TV. In 1996, the U.S. Congress mandated that every television set be equipped with technology that allows parents to block certain shows from being viewed by their children. There is now a system of ratings, similar to the

Bullying in the Media 63

Television shows now have ratings so parents can monitor what their children watch, and the V-Chip was created so that parents could block programs. Above, in 1996, President Bill Clinton (*second from right*) and Vice President Al Gore (*second from left*) met with former Walt Disney Company president Michael Ovitz (*left*) and Westinghouse Electric (now CBS Corporation) chairman and chief executive officer Michael Jordan in 1996 to discuss creating a television ratings system.

system of ratings movies have, to help guide parents in making good choices. However, according to the Parents Television Council, the ratings are applied inconsistently, so some inappropriate programs slip through. In 2007, the Federal Communications Commission, which regulates the media, recommended new legislation that would allow the government to control violence on TV in order to limit young people's exposure to it.

6 BULLYING IN POLITICS AND AT WORK

"If you let a bully come in your front yard, he'll be on your porch the next day. . . ."
—Lyndon B. Johnson (1908-1973), 36th U.S. president

Bullying is not strictly a behavior that young people engage in and then outgrow. Examples of bullying among adults can be found in many parts of society. Nations bully other nations into giving them support for international actions. Politicians running for office try to humiliate each other to gain more votes. Coworkers harass and bully each other to get ahead. It's all part of a culture that values power over cooperation and success over peace.

GOVERNMENTAL BULLYING

Throughout the world and throughout history, governmental leaders have used their power to intimidate citizens who oppose their policies. This often happens in countries with oppressive governments who don't want their citizens to have too many rights.

One example of this is when the South African government enforced the laws of apartheid. Apartheid was a

Critics argue that the South African government tried to bully protestors of apartheid into submission. During the Soweto uprising, protestors rallied against the use of the language Afrikaans in schools—a language that black South Africans associated with apartheid. In this photo, protestors during the uprising use cars as roadblocks on June 21, 1976.

system that separated the races and ethnic groups, and gave whites more rights and power than other groups. Under apartheid, the government attempted to bully antiapartheid activists into submission in a variety of ways. Police shot at protesters to break up rallies. Activists and opposition leaders were taken to jail and held without trial, and sometimes they were tortured until they shared the names and plans of other antiapartheid groups. In essence, the government tried to bully the opposition into giving up and accepting the apartheid state.

One of the most famous incidents was the Soweto Uprising. On June 16, 1976, 10,000 to 15,000 young people in the African township of Soweto staged a peaceful protest for better education. South African security police ordered the crowd to go home, but the people refused. The police released dogs and tear gas and began shooting into the crowd. At least 23 people were killed and more than 100 injured. That was followed by days of less peaceful protests in Soweto and throughout the country. The government hoped their actions would intimidate protesters and stop the antiapartheid movement. Antiapartheid activists refused to back down, and finally, in the 1990s, the apartheid government was dismantled and all races were given equal rights.

Often, oppressive governments will single out individuals whom they see as a threat to their power and try to bully and intimidate them into silence. In Argentina, Jacobo Timerman founded two newspapers that he used as an outlet to report the human rights violations committed by Argentina's government. At this time, the Argentinean government was extremely oppressive and regularly imprisoned and tortured people who spoke out against it. In 1977, the government put Timerman in prison. He was never charged and never had a trial, and while in prison, he was tortured. After a 30-month ordeal, he was exiled to Israel. Despite all this intimidation, Timerman still did not back down. He remained an outspoken journalist outside the country, and in 1984, he returned to Argentina to testify against former military leaders about their human rights violations.

In the world of international diplomacy, leaders of powerful countries often use intimidation to pressure smaller and less powerful countries to do certain things. These leaders can do this by threatening to withhold financial support from or impose trade sanctions on other countries that are dependent on international aid and trade for their economic survival. Sometimes, when a government is violating international law or human rights, these tactics are considered legitimate

Bullying in Politics and at Work

Journalist Jacobo Timerman, seen here in 1994, never backed down against the Argentinean government, which tried to silence him.

diplomatic strategies. However, when governments use these strategies to pressure other countries to do what they want, this is often considered bullying.

The United States is one of the world's foremost "superpowers," meaning that it is a country with a leading position in the international community and it has the ability to influence events and project its power worldwide. Yet, the United States and its leaders have often been accused of acting as an international bully. A 2002 survey of Canadians conducted for *Maclean's* magazine, Global TV Network, and the *Ottawa Citizen* found that almost 70 percent of those surveyed felt that the United States "is starting to act like a bully with the rest of the world."

The Canadian survey was taken when the United States was working to build international support for a military invasion of Iraq. At the time, the United Nations was in the process of inspecting Iraq for evidence of weapons of mass destruction (WMDs). President George W. Bush and other U.S. politicians believed that Iraq was building WMDs and posed a serious security threat to the United States. Bush felt that there was enough evidence of WMDs and that further inspections were not necessary. He argued for a preemptive war—that is, he wanted to attack Iraq before Iraq attacked the United States. However, the leaders of many other countries questioned the necessity of a preemptive war. They wanted to allow the United Nations (U.N.) more time to inspect Iraq for evidence of WMDs and only go to war if all possibilities for diplomacy had been exhausted.

In order for the war to be accepted as legal under international law, the United States needed the backing of the U.N. Security Council. The U.N. Security Council is a coalition of U.N. member nations that vote on resolutions for taking certain military and diplomatic actions. In 2003, the council included some countries that were in favor of the war, some that were opposed, and several that were undecided.

The United States used various tactics to pressure the undecided countries to vote in favor of the war. Many of these tactics involved pressuring smaller countries with fewer resources into supporting the war. This approach was not new. Similar tactics had also been used when the United States was pressing for a U.N. resolution to invade Iraq in 1990. James Baker, the U.S. secretary of state from 1989 to 1992, wrote in his book *The Politics of Diplomacy: Revolution, War and Peace, 1989-1992* that he met personally with undecided members "in an intricate process of cajoling, extracting, threatening, and occasionally buying votes."

In 2003, U.S. representatives threatened to withdraw economic aid to any country that did not support the resolution and promised future aid to countries that did. Some of the countries on the Security Council at the time were extremely poor—including Guinea, Cameroon, and Angola. For these countries, the threat of losing economic assistance from the United States had serious consequences.

Mexico was another country that was very dependent on the United States economically. At first, Mexico's then-president, Vicente Fox, was strongly opposed to the war. But then the U.S. ambassador to Mexico was quoted in the *Washington Post* as saying that, if Mexico voted no, it would lose U.S. cooperation and support on several important issues. And the threat was real: Yemen, a poor Middle Eastern country, voted against the resolution to go to war with Iraq in

Critics of the United States invasion of Iraq in March of 2003 felt U.S. leaders bullied other countries into agreeing to go to war with Iraq. Above, Secretary of State Colin Powell addresses the United Nations Security Council on February 14, 2003 to explain evidence U.S. intelligence had uncovered and to urge other countries to aid in invading Iraq.

DEALING WITH BULLYING

Leaders of some countries, including then-Mexican President Vicente Fox (*left*), did not want to go to war with Iraq, but felt pressured by the U.S. officials to do so. Above, Fox and U.S. President George W. Bush meet in October 2003.

Iraq in 1990 and lost a $70 million aid package. Bush himself was quoted as saying that countries that didn't vote with the United States would face "significant retribution from the government." Soon, Fox began to change this position and move toward supporting the war. In this way, many countries were bullied into supporting the war even though they did not agree with it. These countries' leaders acted out of fear, not because they agreed that invading Iraq was the right thing to do at that time.

Many who were opposed to the war criticized the United States for bullying poorer and less powerful countries into supporting the war. In March 2003, the United States lead Great Britain and several other countries in what it called a "Coalition of the Willing" to invade Iraq. Yet, because the tactics the United States used to gain international support for the war were so well known, the coalition of countries that invaded Iraq has sometimes jokingly been called the "Coalition of the Coerced."

BULLYING IN U.S. POLITICS

Intimidation tactics are often used in U.S. politics. Political bullying may involve pressuring or threatening constituents to vote a certain way or not vote at all, spreading negative rumors about a political candidate, and other tactics. A political action may be considered bullying when it involves intimidating others to ensure a certain outcome. For example, it would be considered political bullying if a politician tries to intimidate another politician to drop out of a race, or a political group tries to intimidate another group not to vote.

As previously discussed, the Ku Klux Klan tried to scare African Americans away from registering to vote in and around the mid-1960s. This type of activity isn't legal, and it would be difficult for any group to get away with such blatant intimidation today. Still, in recent years, some political parties have been accused of trying to stop certain groups of voters from voting in elections. In the 2004 presidential election, there were widespread reports in some states that voters in mostly Democratic precincts were faced with extremely long lines, not enough voting machines, challenges to their registration, and other apparent attempts to stop them from voting, while voters in mostly Republican precincts reportedly faced no such problems. Many believed that these problems were not coincidences; they believed that Republicans had deliberately set things up to stop many Democrats from voting. Even during the 2007 presidential primary, rival candidates Hillary Clinton and Barack Obama accused each other of trying to obstruct voters that were likely to vote for the other candidate in the Nevada primary. These complaints were never proven, but they show that it is possible for political groups to use their power to stop people who oppose them from voting—in other words, bullying people to give up their rights.

Some Democrats believe that state Republican leaders intentionally hindered voting in the 2004 Presidential election in the heavily Democratic parts of key states to gain an advantage. They argue that these tactics included encouraging long lines (such as the one above in Palm Beach County, Florida—a state that was a necessary win in deciding the next president) and not fixing faulty voting machines.

Negative campaigning is another form of bullying in politics. It involves spreading rumors, exposing a candidate's personal life, or using other unfair tactics that focus on the candidate's negative qualities rather than one's own positive qualities. For example, a campaign that produces a TV ad exposing another candidate's personal problems would be considered negative campaigning. Most people agree that such information is not relevant to a candidate's ability to serve in office. Yet, by spreading such negative information, many voters may begin to see that candidate in a more negative light and decide to vote for another candidate—or not at all.

Negative campaigning sometimes involves distorting the truth about a person's position on certain issues or about their qualifications. One of the most famous examples of this is an advertisement by the Lyndon B. Johnson campaign in 1964. The ad showed an innocent child picking a flower and then a fierce mushroom cloud from the explosion of a nuclear bomb. The goal of the ad was to point to Johnson's opponent's military views and make voters feel that opponent Barry Goldwater planned to lead the country to nuclear war. This was an exaggeration of the candidate's position on nuclear war, but it scared voters away from choosing that Goldwater.

Another form of negative campaigning is similar to relational or indirect bullying. Rather than spreading negative information through advertisements, rumors are spread, often over the Internet. For example, during the 2007 presidential primary, a rumor was spread through e-mails that democratic candidate Barack Obama, whose father was born in Kenya, was a Muslim. This tapped into many Americans' post-September 11, 2001 fears about radical Muslim terrorist groups. Although completely unfounded, this information

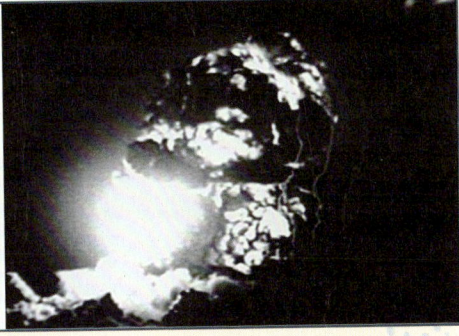

Stills from the Lyndon B. Johnson campaign's famous "mushroom cloud" commercial show a little girl picking flowers followed by the image of a mushroom cloud.

may have been enough to plant a seed of doubt in the minds of some voters about Obama. The e-mail was not traceable, so it is not known who started the rumor.

Because of the damage negative campaigning can do, sometimes candidates try to get another candidate to withdraw by threatening them with personal attacks. When Eugene Wong ran for the San Francisco Board of Supervisors, he met with Walter Wong, a supporter for his opponent and a powerful businessman. According to Eugene Wong, Walter Wong told him that if he didn't withdraw from the race, he would be subject to a smear campaign that would ruin his career as an attorney as well as his run for office. Eugene Wong did not back down though: He filed a complaint with the Ethics Commission and continued his campaign.

Sometimes, even once officials are in office, opponents will try to ruin their career by exposing their personal lives.

NEGATIVE EFFECTS OF NEGATIVE CAMPAIGNING

The goal of negative campaigning is simple: to ensure that the candidate being attacked loses the election. This can be achieved in two ways: First, voters who would have voted for that candidate change their mind and choose another candidate. Second, voters who would have voted for that candidate get so disappointed in him or her that they don't bother to vote at all. Either result means a better chance for the attacking candidate to win the election.

Researchers have investigated whether this strategy works, but the results have not been consistent. Although some studies have found that negative campaigning works to secure more votes for the attacking candidate, other studies have found that negative campaigning actually wins more votes for the candidate who is attacked. This is probably because many voters don't like negative campaigning. When they see a candidate

President Bill Clinton and his wife, Hillary Rodham Clinton, were investigated by the Republican-led House of Representatives and then the Senate from 1994 to 1996 for wrongdoings related to a financial deal known as Whitewater in which the Clintons were involved. No one was ever able to prove that the Clintons did anything wrong, and many Democrats claimed that the Clintons were being treated unfairly by people who wanted to destroy their careers and keep them from accomplishing anything while in office. In other words, the Whitewater investigation was seen as an effort to bully the Clintons out of office.

Because of the unfavorable view that many voters have of negative campaigning, some candidates promise to "take the high road" and stay positive in their campaigns. Barack Obama promised to avoid negative campaigning during his bid for president in 2007. Yet, when his opponent in the using this strategy, they may begin to dislike that candidate and instead choose to vote for someone who keeps his or her campaign positive.

A survey by the Project on Campaign Conduct supported the theory that voters do not like negative campaign strategies. Eighty-seven percent of those who responded to the survey were concerned about the level of personal attacks in campaigns, and 42 percent believe that all candidates purposely make unfair attacks on their opponents. Another study, conducted by Stanford University's Political Communication Lab, also found that negative campaign advertising can give voters a negative view of politics and politicians in general. This is especially true among independent voters who are not loyal to any political party. The study found that voters who are already loyal to a certain candidate or party are less likely to be affected by negative ads. In all, the study concluded that candidates are more likely to get votes by running a positive rather than negative campaign.

Democratic primaries, Hillary Rodham Clinton, began using negative tactics, he had a dilemma. Many commentators in the media suggested that if he did not retaliate or at least respond, he would risk losing the race to be nominated as the Democratic presidential candidate. But if he began to attack Clinton, he would break a campaign promise. In this way, when politicians use negative campaign tactics, they gain power over their rivals by controlling the tone of the race, even if the actual attacks don't change voters' minds.

WORKPLACE BULLYING

Politicians and government leaders aren't the only adults to bully others; bullying is also common among average adult citizens. Whereas bullying among young people generally happens in or around school, bullying among adults often happens at work. A 2007 survey by Zogby International found that 37 percent of adults claim they've been bullied at work.

The Workplace Bullying Institute defines workplace bullying as "repeated, health-harming mistreatment of one or more persons (the targets) by one or more perpetrators." Just like childhood bullying, the workplace bully's actions are driven by the need to control others. They use a variety of tactics to bully their coworkers. They may yell at or insult them, or act in ways that offend, embarrass, or make the victim feel unsafe. Generally, workplace bullies attempt to disrupt a person's ability to get work done or succeed at a job.

The profile of the target of workplace bullying is somewhat different from typical victims of bullying in childhood. Research by the Workplace Bullying Institute has found that typical targets of workplace bullying are workers who are independent and don't like to act submissively. They are often better at their jobs or have better skills than the bully, are well liked, have positive social skills, and are honest and ethical. This is different from childhood bullies, who are often submissive, shy, and insecure.

Similar to childhood bullying, there are different types of workplace bullying and different kinds of bullies. The first type is the most direct form of bullying and is similar to typical schoolyard bullying. The direct workplace bully is short-tempered and has little control over his or her emotions. He or she yells and barks out orders to employees and

WORKPLACE BULLYING LAWS

Unfortunately, dealing with a workplace bully is not always as clear-cut as dealing with a school bully. The Workplace Bullying Institute warns that reporting the bullying to the human resources department or another superior does not usually get results. What's worse, it may lead to an increase in the bullying as the bully tries to get revenge on the victim for speaking out.

Most employers don't have a policy against bullying, and despite the damage workplace bullying can cause, there are no laws against it in the United States. That means that even if an employee speaks up and complains about bullying, their employer doesn't have to do anything about it. Occasionally, a victim has attempted to sue the employer based on grounds other than bullying. For example, in 2005, Joe Doescher sued his employer for emotional distress and assault. He won and was awarded $325,000, but the case remained under appeal for years after the trial. However, because of the lack of a clear law that defines workplace bullying and forces employers to do something about it when it occurs, often the victim's only choice is to leave his or her job to get away from the bullying.

Fortunately, workplace bullying is increasingly being recognized as a serious problem. The Workplace Bullying Institute has led a movement to increase awareness of this problem and push states to enact laws against workplace bullying. As of February 2003, 13 states had introduced an anti-bullying Healthy Workplace Bill. Once passed, these laws should give employees more options when they are faced with a workplace bully.

often loses his or her temper at work. He or she may directly threaten the victim with his or her job.

Another form of workplace bullying may be less obvious to other employees but is just as damaging to the victim. The victim is constantly insulted, criticized, and put down by the bully. He or she may even be wrongly blamed for mistakes that weren't his or her fault. The bully makes unreasonable demands on the person by giving him or her very little time to complete big projects but demanding perfection every time. He or she may also criticize the victim's personal life and generally show no respect for the victim.

The third type of workplace bullying is the most indirect. Like the childhood bully who spreads rumors and works to make sure the victim is excluded or shunned by classmates, the indirect workplace bully works to sabotage his or her victim at work. The Workplace Bullying Institute calls this type of bully the "two-headed snake" because the person pretends to be nice while actually trying to hurt the victim's career. For example, the bully may actively try to gather information that will get the victim fired even if he or she hasn't really done anything wrong. Indirect workplace bullying may also involve actions such as ignoring the victim or excluding him or her from communications (not distributing e-mails or memos to him or her).

Workplace bullying can have severe effects on the victim. Just like childhood bullies, adult victims of bullying can suffer from:

- Stress and stress-related health problems such as trouble sleeping, high blood pressure and heart disease, and reduced immunity (getting sick more often)
- Mental health problems such as depression, low self-esteem, anxiety, and post-traumatic stress disorder
- Career problems—victims of workplace bullying may be forced to quit their jobs because of the bullying,

or the bully may cause them to be transferred or fired

Just like school bullying, if workplace bullying is accepted and no one speaks out against it, it can create a negative, unsafe feeling for everyone at the organization. Workplace bullying can also make it harder for a company to succeed because the stress of bullying distracts workers from doing their jobs. It also leads to more staff quitting their jobs and taking sick time to get away from the bullying.

7 CHANGING THE BULLYING CULTURE AT YOUR SCHOOL

> "If you just start, and other people see what you're doing, they want to join, so it begins to grow. It just takes some guts to make that start, to begin the chain reaction."
>
> —Nickole Evans, community activist

By now you understand the negative effects of bullying—not only for children and teens but for everyone in society. Bullying hurts many people: the victims, the bullies, and everyone around them. When bullying is accepted, it contributes to a negative culture in a school or community—one where aggression and fear rule instead of safety, respect, and friendship. You can learn how to help fight the culture that accepts and promotes bullying and fighting in your school, and help make your school a safe place where everyone feels valued and respected.

There are many elements that go into creating a safe and caring school environment. Everyone plays a role—school staff, teachers, parents, and students. When these groups work together, even schools riddled with bullying and fighting can be transformed into safe, caring communities.

TAKING RESPONSIBILITY

In order to create a safe, caring community, all members—including you—must take responsibility. A person who is responsible is accountable for what he or she does. He or she won't blame others for his or her mistakes. Someone who is irresponsible doesn't care about the consequences of his or actions. He or she may blame others or deny doing something against the rules rather than take responsibility for actions.

Taking responsibility for bullying in your community or school means that you understand that bullying is not just the problem of the bully and the bullied. Even if you've never been picked on, bullying is a community problem, and everyone in the community is responsible for it. That doesn't mean bullying is your fault. It does mean that if you witness bullying, it's your responsibility to do something—either by speaking out against the bully, stepping in to protect the victim (if it's safe), or reporting the bullying to an adult. Don't assume that someone else will take care of it—what if everyone assumed that? Nothing would happen, and the bullying would continue. Take action. The greater the number of voices speaking out against bullying, the more likely you will be heard.

Taking responsibility for bullying can also mean getting involved in improving a school's climate in other ways. What follows is an outline of some ways you can do that.

SHOW EVERYONE RESPECT

In a safe community, everyone is treated with respect. Having respect means that you accept that other people may have different opinions and points of view from yours. Respect is about tolerating those differences. That means that, even if you don't like someone or what someone is doing, you remember that each individual is a human being with the right to be treated with dignity. Nobody—not even a bully—deserves to be ridiculed, insulted, or humiliated.

A respectful school climate is one where *everyone* treats *everyone* with respect. This means that teachers should not purposely embarrass students for not doing work or misbehaving in class. Coaches should not humiliate team members for not playing their best. And students should not tease, taunt, shove, or purposely embarrass other students. In a respectful school, people are considerate of each other's feelings, and they follow the "golden rule": Treat others how they would want to be treated.

INTOLERANCE IS INTOLERABLE

Another important element of a safe community is tolerating differences. This means that everyone is treated with respect regardless of race, ethnicity, religion, weight, hair color, physical ability or disability, or any other difference. Whether you live in a diverse community with students from many different ethnic and religious backgrounds or a community where most people share a similar background, it's important to respect and tolerate those who are different from you.

When differences are not tolerated, this is called prejudice, and prejudice can lead to hate crimes—harassment or violence against someone because of his or her membership in a certain group. Someone who bullies another person because of his or her religion or racial or ethnic background is committing a hate crime. According to Partners Against Hate (www.partnersagainsthate.org), hate crimes have an even stronger impact than "regular" bullying because they make every member of the victim's group feel threatened. Many states, communities, and schools have laws or policies specifically addressing hate crimes, and many communities are working to promote tolerance for diversity to combat prejudice and hate.

As a high school student in Iowa, Robert Perrin-Hayes learned about bullying and hate crimes firsthand. When he was a sophomore in high school, he had to give a speech about bravery for a public-speaking class. In order to illustrate his points about bravery, he decided to reveal that he was gay in the speech. The news of his announcement spread quickly throughout the school and bullying soon followed.

Fellow students called him names, shoved him, and even tried to run him off the road.

Rather than retreat or withdraw from school, Perrin-Hayes took action to keep himself and other students safe from this type of treatment. He began to work with political activists and other teens to convince state officials to pass a Safe Schools bill that would protect students from bullying. By the time Robert was a senior in high school, the bill had passed. Although Robert didn't benefit from the protections offered by the bill because he was graduating, he told a reporter that he felt relieved that "there is actually a chance for everybody to be treated equally."

Prejudice is often the result of ignorance—not understanding and/or fearing something unfamiliar. Taking the time to get to know people as individuals can go a long way in reducing ignorance and prejudice. For example, Jack, who uses a wheelchair, begins to attend a new school. Jane has never met a person in a wheelchair before, and she assumes that Jack isn't as smart as "regular" kids and doesn't want to have fun in the same ways that other kids do. But when she is paired with Jack on a science project, she learns that he's actually just like the other kids she knows. The only difference is how he gets around. Jane and Jack become friends. Jane has learned an important lesson in life: not to make assumptions about people based on how things look on the outside.

Instead of fearing differences, acknowledge, celebrate, and respect the diversity in your school and community. Participate in activities in your school and community that celebrate diversity. Attend cultural events of groups other than your own. For example, attend a festival celebrating Cinco de Mayo, Mexico's Independence Day, even if you are not Mexican.

Become more aware of stereotypes. Stereotypes are oversimplified images or beliefs about groups of people. For example, assuming that all doctors are men is a common stereotype. Instead of making assumptions about members of any group, take the time to get to know people as individuals and learn about their background. Or, you can even read up, on the Internet or at your library, about different groups represented at your school. Just make sure you use reliable sources for your information—ask your librarian for help finding information.

In the same way that keeping silent about bullying sends the message that bullying is okay, keeping silent about prejudice sends the message that prejudice and intolerance is okay. Speak out against intolerance that you see around your school. If you notice a friend stereotyping others with information you know is false, correct him or her. If someone you know insults members of another group, speak up—even if the conversation is private or the person is joking. Let him or her know that prejudice is not funny and that it's not okay with you. You may not change the person's mind, but at least

TAKE ACTION: START AN ANTI-PREJUDICE CLUB

If prejudice and intolerance is a problem in your school, one way to fight them is to start a student anti-prejudice club to stand up for tolerance and diversity. These clubs are sometimes called antibias clubs or even civil rights clubs, and they can make a big difference in changing school climates. Antibias groups help coordinate activities in the school to celebrate diversity, such as international dinners, showing movies about different types of families, and inviting parents and students to share their cultures at school assemblies. They can also provide support and resources for students experiencing bullying because of prejudice.

One civil rights group in Maine had a suggestion box where students could let the team know about things of concern. A student dropped a note in the box after he had witnessed two brothers being bullied on the school bus because of their old, out-of-style clothing. The civil rights team reported the information to the principal, who reported it to the bus driver, who had been unaware of the bullying. The team also sent a note to the brothers telling them that they were sorry about how they

Changing the Bullying Culture at Your School

you've sent the message that you think what he or she said or did is wrong. Plus, you may just make a person think twice about his or her attitude.

COMPASSION IS KEY

Showing compassion means showing others that you care about their feelings. Young people can help build a caring school climate in many ways. Often it's the "little things" that make a difference when it comes to caring. There are many small ways you can show compassion to other kids.

Be nice to the new kids. Moving to a new place and/or starting a new school can be really difficult. It means leaving old friends and teachers behind and starting over. If your new classmates aren't welcoming, it's easy to become isolated—and that makes the new kid an easy target for

had been treated. The bullying was quickly stopped—and the victims knew that other students in school did care about them and believed they deserved to be treated with respect.

Partners Against Hate (www.partnersagainsthate.org) suggests these steps for starting an anti-prejudice club at your school:

- Decide on your guiding principles. Why is it important that your school have an anti-prejudice club? Why is it important to you?
- Get support from other students and teachers who share your concerns. Define your goals as a group, and seek school-wide support.
- Ask a teacher to be your advisor. Look for ways to integrate anti-prejudice messages into the school's curriculum and activities.
- Develop programs and activities for your group, and keep recruiting members.

bullying. Remember actor Tom Cruise, who changed schools 15 times and was bullied at every school he attended. How different might his childhood have been if some of the students in those schools were a little more welcoming?

When you see a new kid at school, take a moment to introduce yourself. Offer to show him or her around. Invite him or her to eat lunch at your table or shoot hoops with you and your friends after school. Even if the person seems unfriendly at first, give him or her a chance. He or she may be shy or may be trying to seem "cool" to hide loneliness or nervousness. You'll probably make his or her day by being friendly—and you may just end up with a new friend yourself.

Simple activities can help people consider their everyday, hurtful actions. Above, Abby Frenzen (*center*) of STOP Violence, a Kansas City-based anti-violence organization, places labels on eighth-grade students' foreheads at Allen Edison Charter School in Kansas City, Missouri. Students then make comments to one another based on their labels, and each student tries to guess what his or her label says.

"Pay it forward." If someone is kind to you, turn around and show someone else a little kindness. This could be as simple as smiling or saying "hello" to someone you don't know in the hallway, sharing your lunch with someone who forgot theirs, or loaning someone a pencil before a big test. Spread the word that kindness is cool by being kind yourself. And when your peers see you acting this way, they just may follow your lead and show someone else a little kindness too.

Make a point to be nice to victims of bullying, too. If you know a classmate is being bullied, take time to be kind to that person. Walk home from school with him or her. Remember that being alone makes it easy for a bully to target a victim, but when friends stick together, bullies often don't even bother. You don't have to be the person's best friend, but showing that you care about his or her safety, and that you believe he or she deserves to be treated well, can mean a lot.

LEARN ABOUT CONFLICT RESOLUTION AND PEER MEDIATION

In order to curb school violence, many schools have conflict resolution programs in place. Conflict resolution is when two people work together to solve a disagreement without violence. The goal of conflict resolution programs is to teach students how to solve problems without fighting; this approach helps reduce aggression and violence in schools.

Many experts warn that conflict resolution isn't always appropriate for dealing with bullying. This is because, as previously explained, bullying is not "normal conflict" in which two people of equal status disagree about something. Bullying is about power, aggression, and victimization. The people involved are not equals, and they don't have a disagreement to resolve.

However, conflict resolution programs are still a key part of any school's overall effort to reduce violence and aggression. Research shows that when conflict resolution programs are put into practice effectively, schools see less violence, better classroom behavior, and improvements in the social and emotional development of students. Remember that both bullies and victims lack effective social skills; conflict resolution programs can help build positive social skills and teach students the importance of treating one another with respect. These skills can help prevent bullying in the first place.

Conflict resolution usually involves learning to do two things: how to listen to another's point of view and how to compromise. In order for conflict resolution to work, everyone involved must be willing to cooperate, or work together to solve the problem. They also need to accept one another's differences and be willing to get creative to solve the problem. A typical conflict resolution process is as follows:

1. Both people calm down and agree to talk things through to solve the problem.
2. Each person explains his or her feelings honestly. Feelings should be expressed honestly but without accusing the other person. A good approach is to use "I" statements. For example, say: "**I** feel hurt that you don't sit with me at lunch anymore" instead of "**You** are so rude. **You** always ignore me now!" The first statement focuses on your feelings. The second statement accuses the other person.
3. Each person listens without interrupting while the other person talks. One technique often taught in conflict resolution program is called active listening. This is when you listen to what the other person says, and when the person is done, you restate what the person says in order to confirm that you understand his or her point of view. Each person should also ask questions to make sure the other side is understood.
4. When both people have expressed their feelings, it's time to start looking for a solution. One way to find creative solutions is to start by brainstorming. Make a list of any idea you both come up with to solve the

WOULD YOU STICK YOUR NECK OUT? THE GIRAFFE HEROES PROJECT

It takes courage to take a stand for something you believe in or to take action to solve a problem in your community. When faced with a problem such as bullying, taking action may mean making some sacrifices. For example, you may risk a place in the popular crowd if you start standing up to kids in that crowd who bully others. Getting involved in an anti-prejudice group or other anti-bullying activities may take up time and energy that you could be spending just enjoying yourself with friends at home, the playground, or the mall. Yet, many people find these risks and sacrifices to be worth it—they even find it satisfying to knowing they are having some impact on a problem that seems important to them to solve.

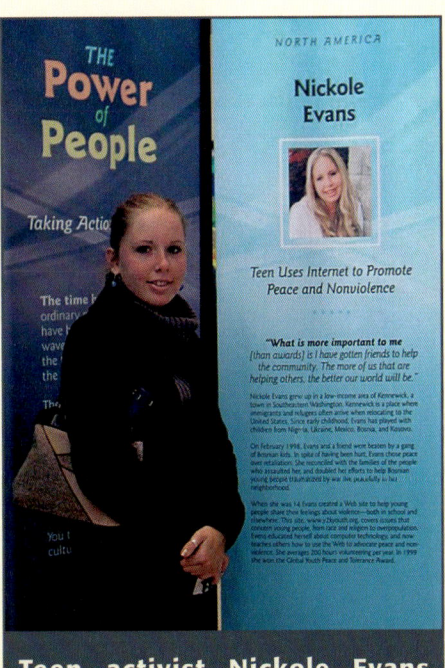

Teen activist Nickole Evans has risked her own safety to spread the message that violence is wrong. Above, she poses in front of a display about her work at the United Nations in 2004.

The Giraffe Heroes Project is a nonprofit organization that recognizes people and adults who stick their neck out for the common good. It tells the stories of these people to inspire others to take action to address challenges they see—in their communities or around the world. The project was started in 1984 by writer, editor, and publisher Ann

(continues)

(continued)

Medlock. She began the project to counter all the violence reported in the media. She collected positive news stories of unknown everyday "heroes"—people who were sticking their neck out for the common good. Since that time, the Giraffe Heroes Project has honored close to a thousand heroes.

Nickole Evans is one such hero. Evans was named a Giraffe Project hero for her work as a teenage community activist. Among her many activities, she is an antiviolence crusader. She started her region's first chapter of Students Against Violence Everywhere (S.A.V.E.), and she has even risked her own safety to educate members of her community about violence. Her community has become home to refugees from many parts of the world that are troubled with war and violence. The children in these families often grew up knowing no other way to solve problems than with violence. When Nickole and a friend were shot with BB guns by some children from Bosnia, she began working in the Bosnian community and talking directly to families and youth about nonviolence. Nickole risked her own safety by going right into the neighborhoods where the kids who shot at her lived in order to spread the message that violence is not a good way to solve problems.

You can find more inspiration from everyday people working for the common good at www.giraffe.org.

problem. While you're making your list, don't evaluate any idea yet. Once both people have compiled a list, review the options one by one. Weigh the pros and cons of each idea. Agree on an idea that works best for both of you. Remember, both sides will probably need to compromise. That means that the solution may not be exactly what you want, but it should be something you can both live with.
5. Once an agreement has been reached, the two people can make a plan for how they'll handle conflict in the future.

Some conflict resolution programs include a mediation component. Mediation means a neutral person works with the people having a disagreement to help them solve the conflict. Often, schools have peer mediators—students specially trained to work with other students to resolve conflicts. Becoming a peer mediator is a great way to contribute to your school's efforts to create a caring, safe, and nonviolent community.

MAKE A DIFFERENCE

Sometimes people hesitate to get involved because they think they're just one person and can't really make a difference in their school or community. But even one person can make a big impact. And when one person takes action, chances are others will follow.

If you're still in doubt, consider the story of a high school in a small community in Nova Scotia, Canada. On his first day of school, a ninth-grade boy wore a pink polo shirt to school. He was taunted by bullies all day. They called him a homosexual and threatened to beat him up. Other students witnessed the bullying, and two 12th-grade boys, David Shepherd and Travis Price, heard about it and decided enough was enough.

David and Travis bought 75 pink T-shirts at a discount store. They spread the word via e-mail to all of their classmates, asking them to wear pink to school the next day or wear one of their pink shirts to support the bullied student. The next day, hundreds of students came to school dressed in pink to show their support. It was a powerful moment when the bullied student walked into school. "Definitely it looked like there was a big weight lifted off his shoulders. He went from looking right depressed to being as happy as can be," David told reporters from the Canadian Broadcast Corporation.

In addition to making the bullied student feel supported, the bullies stopped their bullying in the face of so much anti-bullying sentiment among their peers. "If you can get more people against them . . . to show that we're not going to

92   DEALING WITH BULLYING

Nova Scotia high school students Travis Price (*right*) and David Sheppard (*center*) show Premier Rodney MacDonald their pink shirts in 2007. The Canadian boys bought 75 pink shirts and encouraged students at their school to wear them after a friend was bullied for wearing pink. Their shirts say: "I bought 75 shirts because [of] the story of pink... don't matter!" and "75 pink shirts=$10.00; Gas=$2.00; Defending a GATOR=Priceless!" The second shirt's writing is a play on the popular MasterCard commercials, and the alligator is the mascot of their school.

put up with it and support each other, then they're not as big a group as they think they are," said David.

If such a simple action on the part of two students could have such a big impact in their school, imagine what you and your friends could do about bullying in your school.

GLOSSARY

adrenaline   A hormone secreted by the adrenal gland when a person is stressed or afraid

anxiety disorders   A group of mental illnesses with symptoms of extreme anxiety and fear. Anxiety disorders can be present from an early age, or they can be triggered by a stressful event

anxious   Worried, afraid, uncertain, or nervous

apartheid   A political system in South Africa from 1948 to the 1990s that separated the different racial groups and gave certain rights and privileges only to white people

appreciate   To feel grateful for something

body language   Communication without words (hand gestures, facial expressions, body stance)

bystanders   People who stand by and witness an event

citizen   A member of a community

coerce   To force somebody to do something that he or she doesn't want to do

compromise   When a disagreement is settled by all sides agreeing to accept less than they originally wanted

consumer   Anyone who buys or uses goods or services, including media entertainment

cortisol   A hormone produced by the adrenal gland in response to stress

critical   Being able to study and question something and identify its faults

depression   A mental illness with symptoms of lasting sadness, hopelessness, loss of interest in normal activities, and lack of energy

demeaning   Humiliating someone by reducing them to a much lower status

desensitize   To make somebody less sensitive

dignity   A sense of pride and self-respect

diplomacy The process of communicating and managing relationships between nations

discipline The method adults use to ensure children follow certain rules. Discipline usually involves teaching rules and having consequences for breaking them.

empathy A person's ability to understand how another person feels

ethnic Belonging to a certain group by descent or culture and not by nationality

impulsive Acting on urges without thinking about the consequences first

insecure Lacking self-confidence

intimidate To persuade someone to do or not do something by scaring him or her; for example, by threatening harm to the person or his or her family

legislation Laws passed by the government

media literate Being able to analyze and understand media messages

paranoia Extreme or unreasonable suspicion of other people

passive Not participating actively; letting others make decisions

positive social skills Social skills that help a person get along with others. Positive social skills include cooperation, tolerating differences, and solving conflicts without fighting.

precinct A small area of a city or town

provocative Purposely annoying people or trying to make them angry

self-esteem The way you feel about yourself. A person with high self-esteem values him- or herself; a person with low self-esteem does not value him- or herself.

stereotype An oversimplified image of a group of people that shares certain common traits

submissive Giving in to the demands of others

unique Not like anything else

BIBLIOGRAPHY

Allen, Valerie. "No More Sticks and Stones." *Classroom Management*. September/October 1997.

Anderson, Craig. "Violent Video Games: Myths, Facts, and Unanswered Questions." *Psychological Science Agenda*. October 2003. American Psychological Association Online. Available online. URL: http://apa.org/science/psa/sb-anderson.html. (3/11/08)

"Anxiety Disorders." SAMHSA's National Mental Health Information Center. 2003. Available online. URL: http://mentalhealth.samhsa.gov/publications/allpubs/ken98-0045/default.asp.

Asherman, Jeane. "Decreasing Violence Through Conflict Resolution Education in Schools." Mediate.com: Solutions for Conflict. January 2002. Available online. URL: http://www.mediate.com/articles/asherman.cfm. (3/24/08)

Associated Press. "Columbine lawsuit against makers of video games, movies thrown out." March 5, 2002. Freedom Forum. Available online. URL: http://www.freedomforum.org/templates/document.asp?documentID=15820 (3/11/08)

Azul, Rafael. "Mexico's President Fox Leans Toward US on Iraq." World Socialist Web Site. March 2003. Available online. URL: http://www.wsws.org/articles/2003/mar2003/mex-m14.shtml. (3/13/08)

Baker, James A., III. *The Politics of Diplomacy: Revolution, War and Peace, 1989–1992*. New York: G.P. Putnam's Sons, 1995.

Bardsley, Garth. "Anti-Bullying Activist Robert Perrin-Hayes: You Need to Know Me." MTV.com. July 5, 2007. Available online. URL: http://www.mtv.com/news/articles/156124/20070705/id_0.jhtml. (11/5/07)

Bean, Allen. *The Bully-Free Classroom*. Free Spirit Publishing, 1999.

"Believe It or Not . . . I was Bullied." *US Magazine*, page 77. September 22, 2008.

Berger, Kathleen. "Update on Bullying at School: Science Forgotten?" *Developmental Review* 27 (2007): 90–126.

Bonds, Maria. "Bully-Proofing Your Middle School." *Middle Matters.* Spring 2000.

Bright, Martin, Ed Vulliamy, and Peter Beaumont. "Revealed: US dirty tricks to win vote on Iraq war." *The Observer.* March 2, 2003.

"Bullied student tickled pink by schoolmates' T-shirt campaign." Canadian Broadcast Corporation News. September 19, 2007. Available online. URL: http://www.cbc.ca/canada/nova-scotia/story/2007/09/18/pink-tshirts-students.html (3/25/08)

"Bullies: Innocent Bystanders." PBS Kids. 2005. Available online. URL: http://pbskids.org/itsmylife/friends/bullies/print_article5.html. (3/6/08)

"Bullies: Who's a Target." PBS Kids. 2005. Available online. URL: http://pbskids.org/itsmylife/friends/bullies/article3.html. (1/17/08)

Bullying Facts and Statistics. National Youth Violence Prevention Resource Center. Available online. URL: http://www.safeyouth.org/scripts/faq/bullying.asp. (1/13/08)

Bullying—For Girls. Girlshealth.gov. September 2007. Available online. URL: http://www.girlshealth.gov/bullying/stopping.school.htm. (2/26/08)

Bystanders and Bullying: A summary of research for anti-bullying week. Anti-Bullying Alliance. Available online. URL: http://www.anti-bullyingalliance.org.uk. (3/6/08)

"Bystanders Can Stop Bullying." National Crime Prevention Council. Available online. URL: http://www.ncpc.org/topics/by_audience/parents/bullying/bystanders/ (3/6/08)

Carrier, Jim. *Ten Ways to Fight Hate: A Community Response Guide.* Southern Poverty Law Center, 2005.

The Changing Workplace. Available online. URL: http://www.worktrauma.org/change/change.html. (3/18/08)

"Children and TV Violence." American Academy of Child and Adolescent Psychiatry. November 2002. Available online.

URL: http://www.aacap.org/cs/root/facts_for_families/children_and_tv_violence. (3/11/08)

Components of Developing a Successful School-Based Anti-Bias Club or Program. Partners Against Hate. Available online. URL: http://www.partnersagainsthate.org. (3/20/08)

"Crackdown on schoolgirl bullying epidemic." *The Observer.* January 20, 2008. Available online. URL: http://observer.guardian.co.uk/uj_news/story/0,,2243671,00.html. (1/24/08)

Dehaan, Laura. "Bullies." North Dakota State University Agriculture and University Extension. February 1997. Available online. URL: http://www.ag.ndsu.edu/pubs/yf/famsci/fs570w.htm. (12/05/07)

Do Negative Campaign Ads Work? ThisNation.com. 2004. Available online. URL: http://www.thisnation.com/question/031.html. (3/13/08)

Farhi, Paul, and Frank Ahrens. "FCC Seeks to Rein in Violent TV Shows." *Washington Post.* April 24, 2007. Available online. URL: http://www.washingtonpost.com/wp-dyn/content/article/2007/4/24.htm. (3/11/08)

Field, Evelyn. "Social Survival Skills—Develop Social Resilience." Bully Blocking. Available online. URL: http://www.bullying.com/.au/social-survivor-skills/. (2/26/08)

Geiger, Tasha, Melani L. Zimmer-Gembeck, and Nicki Crick. "The Science of Relational Aggression: Can we guide intervention?" in *Girls and Aggression: Contributing Factors and Intervention Principles.* New York: Springer, 2004.

The Giraffe Heroes Project. 2007. Available online. URL: http://www.giraffe.org. (3/19/07)

Goldman, Linda. "Nowhere Feels Safe: The Bullying Epidemic." *Healing Magazine.* 2008. Available online. URL: http://www.kidspeace.org/healingMagazine/NewHealing.healing_fw05_6.htm. (1/24/06)

Green Party. "US Constitution Mandates Penalties for States Where Votes Are Obstructed." Green Party of the United States. December 16, 2004. Available online. URL: http://www.gp.org/press/pr_2004_12_16.html. (3/16/08)

Greenway, Norma. "Most See U.S. as a 'Bully,' Survey Finds. *The Ottawa Citizen*. December 31, 2002.

Harris, Scott. "Washington Bribes, Threatens and Spies on Nations to Coerce Support for U.S. War on Iraq." Between the Lines. March 10, 2003. Available online. URL: http://www.scoop.co/nz/stories/HL0303/S00069.htm. (3/13/08)

Healy, Patrick, and Julie Bosman. "Clinton Campaign Starts 5-Point Attack on Obama." *The New York Times*. February 26, 2008. Available online. URL: http://www.nytimes.com/2008/02/26/us/poliics/26clinton.html. (3/18/08)

"Help for Bullies." Stop Bullying Now! Available online. URL: http://www.stopbullyingnow.com/interven2.htm. (12/05/07)

"Helping Kids Deal with Bullies." KidsHealth. Available online. URL: http://www.kidshealth.org/parent/emotions/behavior/bullies.html. (2/26/08)

Herel, Suzanne. "Political Bullying Alleged: District 3 Candidate Claims Intimidation." *San Francisco Chronicle*. September 8, 2004. Available online. URL: http://www.sfgate.com/cgi-bin/article.cgi?f=/c/a/2004/09/08/BAGN68L64D1.DTL. (3/16/08)

Hobbs, Renee. "Teaching Media Literacy: Yo! Are You Hip to This?" Center for Media Literacy. 2007. Available online. URL: http://www.medialit.org/reading_room/article211.html. (3/11/08)

Holmes, Steven. "Mayoral candidates' campaign ads reflect their different styles." *The New York Times*. November 5, 1989. Available online. URL: http://query.nytimes.com/gst/fullpage.html?res=950DE6D9173BF936A35752C1A96F948260. (3/17/08)

"How Is Depression Different from Regular Sadness?" KidsHealth. 2007. http://www.kidshealth.org/teen/your_mind/mental_health_depression/html. (12/05/07)

"How to Deal with a Bullying Problem." Reader's Digest Canada. Available online. URL: http://www.readersdigest.ca.mag/2001/10/bullyingexpert.html. (2/26/08)

Bibliography

How to Help Someone Being Bullied. BullyingUK. Available online. URL: http://www.bullying.co.uk/pupils/howtohelp.aspx. (2/26/08)

Inger, Morton. "Conflict Resolution Programs in Schools." Eric/Cue Digest Number 74. June 1991. Available online. URL: http://www.ericdigests.org/1992-5/conflict.htm. (3/24/08)

Iyengar, Shanto. "Going Negative." Stanford University Political Communication Lab. Available online. URL: http://pcl.stanford.edu/common/docs/research/iyengar/1996/goingneg.html. (3/18/08)

Iyenger, Shanto. "Negative Ads Turnoff Voters, Enthrall News Media." WashingtonPost.com. November 15, 2006. Available online. URL: http://www.washingtonpost.com/wp-dyn/content/article/2006/11/15/AR2006111500827.html. (3/18/08)

Jacobsen, Kristen. "Bullying in Schools: School counselors' responses to three types of bullying incidents." Professional School Counseling. October 2007. Available online. URL: http://findarticles.com/p/articles/mi_moKoC/is_1_11/ai_n21093605. (1/09/08)

Jaffe, Elisa. "State Lawmakers Consider Law Against Workplace Bullies." Seattle: KOMO TV 4. November 1, 2007. Available online. URL: http://www.workplacebullyinglaw.org/press/komotv110107.html. (3/18/08)

Journal of the American Medical Association. "Early Home Environment and Television Watching Influence Bullying Behavior." *ScienceDaily*. April 21, 2005. Available online. URL: http://www.sciencedaily.com/releases/2005/04/05042009955.htm. (3/11/08)

Kass, Jeff. "Witnesses Tell of Columbine Bullying." Rocky Mountain News. October 3, 2000. Available online. URL: http://www.denver-rmn.com/shooting/1003co14.shtml. (12/05/07)

"Keeping Kids Healthy in a 24/7 Media World." Common Sense Media. 2007.

Maag, Christopher. "A Hoax Turned Fatal Draws Anger but No Charges." *The New York Times*. 11/28/07. Available online.

URL: http://www.ntytimes.com/2007/11/28/us/28hoax.html. (1/09/08)

Mackay, Scott. "Pros and cons of negative campaign tactics." *The Providence Journal.* January 30, 2008.

Marano, Hara Estroff. "Big Bad Bully." *Psychology Today.* Sept/Oct 1995. http://psychologytoday.com/articles/index.php?term=pto-19950901-000020&print=1. (1/24/08)

Olweus, Dan. *Bullying at School.* Malden, Mass.: Blackwell Publishing, 1993.

Payne, January. "More Effort Urged to Stop Bullying." AZCentral.com. August 25, 2005. Available online. URL: http://www.azcentral.com/health/kids/articles/0825bully-ON.html. (1/15/08)

Phillips, Helen. "Effects of bullying worse for teens." *New Scientist.* October 2004. Available online. URL: http://www.newscientist.com/article/dn6600-effects-of-bullying-worse-for-teens.html. (12/05/07)

Political Scandals. CBS News. Available online. URL: http://www.cbsnews.com/elements/2003/11/20/in_depth_politics/whoswho584748.shtml. (3/18/08)

Positive Change Through Policy: Hate Crimes. National Crime Prevention Council. Available online. URL: http://www.ncpc.org/publications/available-online/home-and-neighborhood-safety/positive-change-through-policy. (3/20/08)

Pytel, Barbara. "Long-Term Effects of Bullying." August 17, 2006. Available online. URL: http://educationalissues.suite101.com/article.cfm/long_term_effects_of_bullying. (12/05/07)

Reducing Bullying: Meeting the Challenge. The Melissa Institute for Violence Prevention and Treatment. Available online. URL: http://www.teachsafeschools.org/bullying-prevention2.html. (3/20/08)

Rogow, Faith. "ABCs of Media Literacy: What Can Preschoolers Learn?" Center for Media Literacy. Available online. URL: 2007. http://www.medialit.org/reading_room/article566.html. (3/11/08)

Safety & Health Assessment and Research for Prevention Program. Workplace Bullying: What Everyone Needs to Know. Washington State Department of Labor and Industries Report # 87-1-2006. August 2006.

"The School Bully Can Take a Toll on Your Child's Mental Health." SAMHSA's National Mental Health Information Center. November 2003. Available online. URL: http://mentalhealth.samhsa.gov/publications/allpubs/Ca-0043/default.asp. (12/05/07)

"School Bullying Is Nothing New, but Psychologists Identify New Ways to Prevent It. *Psychology Matters.* American Psychological Association Online. 2007. Available online. URL: http://www.psychologymatters.org/bullying.html. (12/05/07)

Sommerfield, Julia. "Seattle Study of Kids Links Bullying to TV." *The Seattle Times.* April 5, 2005. Available online. URL: http://seattlctimes.nwsource.com/html/education/2002231136_bullying05m.html. (3/11/08)

Smith, Ben, and Jonathan Martin. "Untraceable emails spread Obama rumor." Politico. October 15, 2007. Available online. URL: http://www.politico.com/news/stories/1007/6314.html. (3/17/08)

Smith, Donna. "Inside the Mind of a Bully: An Interview." Children Today. Available online. URL: http://childrentoday.com/resources/articles/bullies3.html. (1/17/08)

Smith, Marylyn E. "Television Violence and Behavior: A Research Summary." ERIC Digest. December 1993. Available online. URL: http://www.ericdigests.og/1994/television.htm. (3/11/08)

Snyder, Marlene. "Understanding Bullying and Its Impact on Kids with Learning Disabilities or AD/HD." Charles and Helen Schwab Foundation. 2003. Available online. URL: http://www.schwablearning.org/articles.aspx?r=692. (1/13/08)

"Sticks, Stones and Bullies." CBS News Online. March 23, 2005. Available online. URL: http://www.cbc.ca/includes/printablestory.jsp. (3/11/08)

Stop Bullying Now! Effects of Bullying. U.S. Department of Health and Human Services. Available online. URL: http://stopbullyingnow.hrsa.gov/index.asp?area=effects. (1/09/08)

Stop Bullying Now! "What We Know About Bullying." U.S. Department of Human Services. Available online. URL: http://stopbullyingnow.hrsa.gov.

"Stories About Bullying." Bully B'ware. Available online. URL: http://www.bullybetare.com/story.html. (1/09/08)

The Story of U.S. Legislative Advocacy. The U.S. Campaign for Workplace Bullying Laws. 2008. Available online. URL: http://www.bullyfreeworkplace.org/id29.html. (3/18/08)

"Stress: Unhealthy response to the pressures of life." MayoClinic.com. 2006. Available online. URL: http://www.mayoclinic.com/health/stress/SR00001. (12/05/07)

"Study: Gifted children especially vulnerable to effects of bullying." Purdue University News. April 6, 2006. Available online. URL: http://www.purdue.edu/UNS/html4ever/2006/060406>Peterson.bullies.html. (12/05/07)

"Sugar and Spice and Everything Nice? That's not what some girls are made of." University of Minnesota College of Education and Human Development. 2007. Available online. URL: http://cehd.umn.edu/Pubs/ResearchWorks/Crick.html. (1/27/08)

Szymanski, Tekla. "Jacobo Timerman: Uncompromising Journalist." *World Press Review.* January 2000.

"Take Action Against Bullying." SAMHSA's National Mental Health Information Center. 2003. Available online. URL: http://mentalhealth.samhsa.gov/publications/allpubs/SVP-0056/. (1/13/08)

"This Honorable Court: Court Cases Brought by Bullied Students." Raven Days. Available online. URL: http://www.ravendays.org/court.html. (12/05/07)

U.S. Arm-Twisting. Global Policy Forum. Available online. URL: http://www.globalpolicy.org/security/issues/iraq/attack/armtwistindex.htm. (3/13/08)

U.S. Secret Service and U.S. Department of Education. The Final Report of the Safe School Initiative. Washington, D.C. May 2002.

VanNuys, Melanie. "The Bully Spectrum." Preteenagers Today. Available online. URL: http://www.preteenagerstoday.com/articles/1100. (1/17/08)

"Violent Video Games Can Increase Aggression." April 23, 2000. American Psychological Association. Available online. URL: http://www.apa.org/releases/videogames.html.

Webb, Patrick. "Beliefs and Bullying: Factors Associated with Peer Victimization Among Youth." ERIC. October 2006. Available online. URL: http://www.eric.ed.gov/ERICWebPortal/custom/portlets/recordDetails/detailmini.jsp?_nfpb=true&_&ERICExtSearch_SearchValue_0=ED493749&ERICExtSearch_SearchType_0=no&accno=ED493749. (3/24/08)

Wessler, Stephen L. *The Respectful School.* Alexandria, Va.: Association for Supervision and Curriculum Development, 2003.

"What Can You Do to Prevent Bullying in Your School?" Girlshealth.gov. Available online. URL: http://www.girlshealth.gov/bullying/stopping.school.htm. (2/26/08)

"What Is Cyberbullying, Exactly?" Stop Cyberbullying. Available online. URL: http://www.stopcyberbullying.org/what_is_cyberbullying_exactly.html. (1/13/08)

"When Your Child Is a Bully." National Crime Prevention Council. Available online. URL: http://www.ncpc.org/topics/by-audience/parents/bullying/when-your-child-is-a-bully.

Willard, Nancy. "Parent Guide to Cyberbullying and Cyberthreats." 2007. Available online. URL: http://www.cyberbully.org/cyberbully/bcbook/php. (1/13/08)

The Workplace Bullying Institute Web Site. Available online. URL: http://bullyinginstitute.org. (3/18/08)

World, Heather. "Getting Beyond Bullying." *Children's Advocate.* September-October 2002. Action Alliance for Children. Available online. URL: http://www.4children.org/news/902/bulle.htm. (1/24/08)

FURTHER RESOURCES

BOOKS

Beard, Candy J. *Please Don't Cry, Cheyenne.* PublishAmerica, 2007.

Humphrey, Sandra Mcleod. *Hot Issues, Cool Choices: Facing Bullies, Peer Pressure, Popularity, and Put-downs.* Prometheus Books, 2007.

Knapp, J. Richard. *Bobby's Story.* Thornton Publishing, 2006.

Schwartz, Susan, *Coping with Cliques: A Workbook to Help Girls Deal with Gossip, Put-downs, Bullying, and Other Mean Behavior.* New Harbinger, 2008.

Slavens, Elaine. *Bullying: Deal with It Before Push Comes to Shove.* Lorimer, 2003.

Winkler, Kathleen. *Bullying: How to Deal with Taunting, Teasing, and Tormenting.* Enslow Publishers, 2005.

WEB SITES

McGruff
http://www.mcgruff.org
The National Crime Prevention Council's anti-bullying Web site for young people. Includes games, advice, and more.

PACER Center's Kids Against Bullying
http://www.pacerkidsagainstbullying.org
Includes games, polls, and contests about putting a stop to bullying.

Stop Bullying Now!
http://stopbullyingnow.hrsa.gov
The U.S. Department of Health and Human Services Web site about bullying for young people.

PICTURE CREDITS

Page:

- 15 Angela Hampton Picture Library/Alamy
- 19 AP Images
- 21 ©Infobase Publishing
- 23 George Skene/MCT/Landov
- 33 Newscom
- 37 Lester Cohen/Newscom
- 49 Mika Fuentes/MCT/Landov
- 51 AP Images
- 56 Newscom
- 58 Newscom
- 61 Newscom
- 63 Wilfredo Lee/AP Images
- 65 Hulton Archive/Newscom
- 67 Newscom
- 69 Newscom
- 70 Newscom
- 72 Newscom
- 73 LBJ Library and Museum
- 86 Newscom
- 89 Courtesy of Nickole Evans
- 92 Communications Nova Scotia/Michael Creagen

INDEX

A
acne, 22
adults
    bullying among, 64–79
aggressive
    behavior, 27, 29, 55–57, 59, 62, 80
    relational, 30
Aguilera, Christina, 34, 37
alcohol and drug use
    after bullying, 20, 23–24
American Academy of Child and Adolescent Psychiatry, 55, 57
American Idol (television show), 57
America's Funniest Home Videos (television show), 57
Anderson, Craig, 59
anti-bullying programs, 48
    legislation, 49–50, 77, 83
    spokespeople, 28, 89
anti-prejudice clubs, 84–85
anxiety disorders, 22, 25, 78
Argentina, 66
asthma attacks, 22
attention deficit disorder (ADD), 38
attention deficit/ hyperactivity disorder (AHDD), 46

B
Bale, Christian, 37
Baker, James, 68
Banks, Tyra, 34, 37
body image, 43
body language, 42
bullies
    encouragement, 54
    handling, 45–46, 48
    harm to, 14, 22–24, 80
    help for, 31
    home life of, 26–27, 30–31
    needs, 26
    reactive, 28–29
    reformed, 28
    understanding, 25–31
Bully B'ware productions, 18, 20
bullying
    attitudes about, 13
    behavior, 13
    court cases, 30, 77
    dealing with, 41–53
    defined, 14–17
    and the law, 49–50, 77–79
    in the media, 54–63
    in politics, 64–76
    prevention, 28, 31, 40
    research, 14, 16, 18, 20, 23–28, 30–32, 34–36, 39, 41, 55
    tragic results of, 13, 16, 18–20
    types of, 17–19, 29–31, 47, 76–77
    in the workplace, 64, 76–79
Bully Police USA, 50
Bush, George W., 68, 70
bystanders
    and bullying, 14, 24, 48, 50, 52–54
    passive, 50–51
    research, 48

C
Center for Safe and Responsible Internet Use, 47
Chaney, James, 52
Children and Adults with Attention-Deficit/ Hyperactivity Disorder (CHADD), 39
Civil Rights movement, 51–52, 84
Clinton, Bill, 34, 37, 75

Index

Clinton, Hillary Rodham, 71, 75–76
"Coalition of the Coerced," 71
"Coalition of the Willing," 70
Columbine High School shooting, 16, 59
Common Sense Media, 55–56
compassion, 85–87
confidence
    acting, 41–43
    need for, 25
conflict, 29
    defined, 14–17
    resolutions, 60, 62, 87–88, 90–91
Crick, Nicki, 30–31
Cruise, Tom, 37, 86
cyberbullying (online bullying)
    examples of, 17–19, 47

D
depression, 19, 22, 91
Dickens, Charles
    Oliver Twist, 14
different
    ethnic and cultural, 34, 81–84
direct bullying, 17, 24, 29–30
    and bystanders, 50
Doescher, Joe, 77

E
Education, Department of, 13, 16
Emerson, Ralph Waldo, 41
Ethics Commission, 74
Evans, Nickole, 90

F
Federal Communications Commission, 63
Fox, Vicente, 69–70
friends
    lack of, 23
    protection against bullying, 20, 31, 44–45

G
getting involved, 43–44
Giraffe Heroes project, 89–90
Goldwater, Barry, 73
Goodman, Andrew, 52
gossiping, 17
Great Britain, 70

H
Harris, Eric, 16, 59
Health and Human Services Department, 18
Healthy Workplace Bill, 77
Houston, Whitney, 37
Humanitas Prize, 61

I
indirect bullying
    examples of, 17, 30, 39, 53, 73, 78
injustice, 51–52
Institute of Child Health and Human Development, 18
intolerance, 62, 82–85
iParenting.com, 26
Iraq
    invasions of, 68–71

J
jealousy, 34
Johnson, Lyndon B., 64, 73

K
Klebold, Dylan, 16, 59
Ku Klux Klan, 51–52, 71

L
Ladd, Gary, 32, 34
learning disabilities, 37–39
loneliness, 36
Lovato, Demi, 37

M
Marano, Hara Estroff, 27
media
    bullying in, 16, 28, 54–63
    literate, 58, 60, 62

Medlock, Ann, 89–90
Meier, Megan, 19
mental health problems, 22, 78
Mexico, 69–70
"My Bullying Nearly Killed Her" (television show), 25
MySpace web site, 19

N
National School Safety Security Services, 50
negative campaigning, 72–73
    effects of, 74–75
    research, 75
Nemours Foundations Center for Children's Health Media, 23

O
Obama, Barack, 71, 73–76
Oliver Twist (Dickens), 14
Olweus, Dan
    bullying research, 14, 16, 18, 20, 24–25, 35
online bullying. *see* cyberbullying

P
panic attacks, 22
paranoia, 27, 29
Partners Against Hate, 82, 85
passive personalities, 35–36
Patterson, Gerald, 27
peer
    acceptance, 27, 31, 54
peer mediation, 87–88, 90–91
Perrin-Hayes, Robert, 82–83
Perry, David, 28
phobias, 22
Pieffer, Michelle, 38
politics
    bullying in, 64–76
popularity
    and bullying, 22–23, 25
post-traumatic stress disorder, 22, 78
power and control
    and bullying, 16–17, 23, 26–28

prejudice
    reducing, 28, 62, 83–84
Price, Travis, 91, 92
Project on Campaign Conduct, 75
Psychology Today, 27, 34–35

R
racism, 34, 71
reactive bullies, 29
relational bullying, 17, 29–31
respect, 81–82
responsibility, 81
Rodkin, Philip, 22
rumor
    spreading of, 45, 50, 53, 73, 78

S
Safe Schools Initiative, 16
school
    changing bullying in, 80–92
    shootings, 13, 16
Schwartz, David, 35
Schwerner, Michael, 52
Secret Service, 13, 16
self-esteem
    building, 42, 45
    low, 25, 78
Shepherd, David, 91–92
Singer, Jerome L., 54
sleep disorders, 22, 78
Smith, Donna, 26
social
    isolation, 35–36, 85
    outcasts, 16
    skills, 28
    values, 61
South Africa
    apartheid, 64–65
    government, 64–66
Soweto Uprising, 66
Spivak, Howard, 18
SpongeBob SquarePants (television show), 56, 58
standing up
    for others, 51
    for yourself, 36

stereotyping, 62, 83–84
stress
    physical effects of, 20–22, 78
Students Against Violence Everywhere (S.A.V.E.), 90
Substance Abuse and Mental Health Services Administration (SAMHSA), 24
suicide
    after being bullied, 13, 16, 19–20
    warning signs, 20

T
Timerman, Jacobo, 66
tolerance
    of bullying, 14, 30, 79
    of differences, 81–82
Tufts University, 18

U
United Nations
    resolution, 68–69
    Security Council, 68–69
United States
    government bullying, 67–71
    politics, 71–76

V
victims of bullying
    external characteristics, 32–34, 85
    famous, 34, 37–38
    help for, 40, 44, 50–53
    how it hurts, 14, 16, 18–22, 78, 80
    internal characteristics, 34–36, 38–40
    provocative, 36, 38–40
    reactions, 26, 29, 36, 39–41, 45–46, 53
    understanding, 32–40, 87
video games
    and bullying, 59
    research, 59
violence, 16, 36
    attitudes about, 57
    and crimes, 24
    in the home, 26
    in school, 87
    on TV, 55–58, 60, 62–63

W
weapons of mass destruction, 68
Whitewater scandal, 75
Willard, Nancy, 47
Winslet, Kate, 38
Wong, Eugene, 74
Wong, Walter, 74
Woods, Tiger, 34, 37
workplace
    bullying in, 24, 64, 76–79
    laws, 77–79
Workplace Bullying Institute, 76–78

Z
Zimmerman, Frederick, 55

ABOUT THE AUTHOR AND CONSULTANTS

Alexa Gordon Murphy has an M.A. in professional writing from the University of Massachusetts at Dartmouth. She has written many educational materials on character education and bullying, including interactive presentation kits for teachers and parents and workbooks for elementary, middle school, and high school children. Murphy is a freelance writer and editor. She lives in New England with her husband, children, and pets.

Series consultant **Dr. Madonna Murphy** is a professor of education at the University of St. Francis in Joliet, Illinois, where she teaches education and character education courses to teachers. She is the author of *Character Education in America's Blue Ribbon Schools* and *History & Philosophy of Education: Voices of Educational Pioneers*. She has served as the character education consultant for a series of more than 40 character education books for elementary school children, on the Character Education Partnership's Blue Ribbon Award committee recognizing K-12 schools for their character education, and on a national committee for promoting character education in teacher education institutions.

Series consultant **Sharon L. Banas** was a middle school teacher in Amherst and Tonawanda, New York, for more than 30 years. She led the Sweet Home Central School District in the development of its nationally acclaimed character education program. In 1992, Sharon was a member of the Aspen Conference, drafting the Aspen Declaration that was approved by the U.S. Congress. In 2001, she published *Caring Messages for a School Year*. She has been married to her husband Doug for 37 years. They have a daughter, son, and new granddaughter.